# WILLIAM'S
# MIDSUMMER
# DREAMS

## Also by
# ZILPHA KEATLEY SNYDER

# WILLIAM'S
# MIDSUMMER
# DREAMS

*Zilpha Keatley Snyder*

ATHENEUM BOOKS *for* YOUNG READERS

NEW YORK LONDON TORONTO SYDNEY NEW DELHI

ATHENEUM BOOKS FOR YOUNG READERS

An imprint of Simon & Schuster Children's Publishing Division

1230 Avenue of the Americas, New York, New York 10020

This book is a work of fiction. Any references to historical events, real people, or real locales are used fictitiously. Other names, characters, places, and incidents are products of the author's imagination, and any resemblance to actual events or locales or persons, living or dead, is entirely coincidental.

Copyright © 2011 by Zilpha Keatley Snyder

All rights reserved, including the right of reproduction in whole or in part in any form.

ATHENEUM BOOKS FOR YOUNG READERS is a registered trademark of Simon & Schuster, Inc.

For information about special discounts for bulk purchases, please contact Simon & Schuster Special Sales at 1-866-506-1949 or business@simonandschuster.com.

The Simon & Schuster Speakers Bureau can bring authors to your live event. For more information or to book an event, contact the Simon & Schuster Speakers Bureau at 1-866-248-3049 or visit our website at www.simonspeakers.com.

Also available in an Atheneum Books for Young Readers hardcover edition.

The text for this book is set in Centaur and Gotica Lumina.

Manufactured in the United States of America

0512 OFF

First Atheneum Books for Young Readers paperback edition June 2012

10 9 8 7 6 5 4 3 2 1

The Library of Congress has catalogued the hardcover edition as follows:

Snyder, Zilpha Keatley.

William's midsummer dreams / Zilpha Keatley Snyder. — 1st ed.

p. cm.

Sequel to: William S. and the great escape.

Summary: Now permanently settled with Aunt Fiona, who has adopted him and his siblings, thirteen-year-old William gets the chance to play Puck in a professional production of A Midsummer Night's Dream.

ISBN 978-1-4424-1997-1 (hardcover)

[1. Brothers and sisters—Fiction. 2. Acting—Fiction. 3. Theater—Fiction. 4. Adoption—Fiction. 5. Family problems—Fiction. 6. Aunts—Fiction.] I. Title.

PZ7.S68522Whp 2011 [Fic]—dc22 2010036958

ISBN 978-1-4424-1998-8 (paperback)

ISBN 978-1-4424-1999-5 (eBook)

To the Tuesday group who helped William,
and many more of my characters,
to find their way home—
Ella Ellis, Alla Crone Hayden,
Patsy Garlan, and Gennifer Choldenko

# WILLIAM'S
# MIDSUMMER
# DREAMS

It was on a Saturday near the end of September when the doorbell at 971 Eleanor Street rang long and loud, and then rang again. As William hurried to answer it, a sudden memory caused a shiver to slither up the back of his neck—a sneaky reminder of the time when that same doorbell's impatient ringing turned out to be the first act in a true-to-life tragedy with a cast of three big, angry Baggetts—Big Ed Baggett and two of William's enormous half brothers. Three of the people who had helped to make William's life and the lives of his younger brother and sisters miserable, right up until the four of them had finally managed to escape again to Gold Beach to live with their aunt Fiona Hardison.

*Forget it,* he told himself. *You and Jancy and the kids are legal Hardisons now. Forget the Baggetts.* And he pretty much had. Except for sometimes late at night, when something deep inside his sleeping mind insisted on reminding him.

He shook his head hard. Hard enough, he hoped, to shake away all those persistent memories of his Baggett-haunted past. Then he pulled the door open to reveal . . . just old Sam Miller, the Gold Beach mailman.

Pulling out a big red handkerchief, old Sam mopped his forehead and told William that a large package was waiting to be picked up at the post office. Picked up because there was no package delivery at the Gold Beach post office anymore.

"No use complaining, 'cause that's just the way it is nowadays," Mr. Miller said sternly. "Gov'ment's got no money for delivery vehicles what with this here Depression we're havin'. So if yer package is too big for poor old Sam to lug around, it's up to you to come get it. And this one's a big'un." Then his scowl turned into a grin. "Think it's somethin' for you, kid. Got the name William S. Hardison printed right there next to your auntie's address. Plain as can be."

"Gee," William said. "For me? Are you sure?" He must have sounded pretty surprised, because Mr. Miller grinned again and added that he'd just happened to notice that it had been mailed in Crownfield, but other than that there was no return address.

The fact that Mr. Miller had "just happened" to notice so many things about the package wasn't that much of a surprise. According to Aunt Fiona, Sam Miller's favorite words were "who," "what," and "how much." "Who" had been getting interesting mail, "what" it might be, and even "how much" it cost. And recently one of Mr. Miller's special interests seemed to have been the "whos" and "whys" that lay behind the fact that longtime Gold Beach resident Fiona Hardison had quite suddenly acquired a large family.

Backing up carefully, and swinging the heavy mailbag off his shoulder, solid old Sam settled down on one of Aunt Fiona's wicker porch chairs, making it sag and creak ominously. "Just gonna rest my bones here a minute or two," he said, mopping his forehead again. "So you're not 'spectin' anything, boy? Didn't send off for a basketball or something like that? Package looks 'bout that size."

William shook his head, "No sir, no basketball. Nothing that I know anything about. Nothing at all."

Okay, he'd just had his thirteenth birthday a few days ago, but he'd already received cards from Miss Scott and the Ogdens, and neither of them had said anything about sending a present. The only other people in Crownfield who knew where he was were Baggetts, and the odds against a Baggett sending a present to William S. Hardison were about a zillion to one.

Actually, it wasn't the first time he'd gotten something in the mail since he and Jancy and the two little kids had come to live with Aunt Fiona. There had been one letter from Clarice Ogden. The one that Jancy had made such a fuss about because Clarice had written that she, too, was going to be at Mannsville next summer, and she knew that she and William were going to be <u>very close friends</u>.

Which, according to Jancy, proved that Clarice was in love with him.

Fat chance! Okay, so she did underline "<u>very close friends,</u>" but that didn't mean anything. And the fact that when the four of them were hiding in her basement, she tried so hard to keep them from leaving didn't mean anything either—except that she was an only child, and kind of lonely. And that one letter she'd sent him definitely didn't say anything about sending a package.

As soon as the mailman finally went down the steps, William went looking for Aunt Fiona so he could quietly tell her about the package and ask if he could go downtown right away to pick it up. Quietly, because if Buddy heard, he'd be sure to insist on going too, and that would change a quick half-mile hike into an expedition that would probably take most of the day.

At the moment, Aunt Fiona was sitting at the dining room table getting ready for Columbus Day by attaching a big map to a cardboard frame—a map that showed the route taken by the *Niña* and *Pinta* and *Santa María*. All the kids in her class who wrote an essay about Columbus's voyage were going to get to move their reading group's ship an inch farther along. Aunt Fiona, who was a fourth-grade teacher, was always doing stuff like that.

Meanwhile, Buddy was running in and out of the room holding a toy biplane over his head and yelling, "Zoom-zoom-zoom" at the top of his lungs. And the top of that kid's lungs was right up there with a train's whistle or a really loud clap of thunder. So it was under the cover of earsplitting *zooms* that William managed to have a private discussion with Aunt Fiona. "Mr. Miller says there's a package for me at the post office. I could go pick it up right away. Didn't you want me to get something at the grocery store?"

"Oh yes." Knowing, without being told, why it was important to keep quiet about William's errand, Aunt Fiona waited for the next flight to zoom through and disappear into the living room before she whispered, "Come with me," got up, and led the way to the kitchen, where she washed the paste off her hands and, in the brief moments between incoming flights, wrote out a short list and gave William three dollars. "That ought to cover it," she said. "And you might leave by the back door if you aren't interested in an air force escort."

He liked the subtle way his aunt put things. For instance, saying, "If you aren't interested in an air force escort" instead of something like, "Better sneak out, or you'll get stuck with Buddy." Grinning good-bye, William quietly slid out the back door and, by ducking way down, was able to pass the living room windows without being spotted by his little brother.

And so he was off—striding rapidly toward downtown Gold Beach, without having to answer a lot of "whys" and "whats" and "how comes." Not to mention having to wait while four-year-old Buddy came down to earth long enough to squat down and carefully examine anything on the sidewalk that was the least bit disgusting—like dead stinkbugs, squashed snails, or piles of dog poop. Buddy seemed to have a special interest in that sort of thing, especially dog poop, where he usually wanted to discuss how big a dog had done it, and how long ago.

But now, as William walked rapidly down Eleanor Street with no questions to answer or sidewalk messes to inspect, he was able to let his mind roam on ahead of him. He thought about the package, of course, about what it might be and who could have sent it.

But after a while he began to think of other things. Like the argument he'd had that morning with Jancy. As a rule he didn't have arguments with his sister, at least not very serious ones. Not even when she said really stupid things, like insisting that Clarice Ogden was in love with him. But this morning, while they were doing the breakfast dishes, she just seemed to be in a bad mood.

He didn't know what could have set her off. All he'd done was to mention something about next summer, when he might be living on a college campus near San Francisco for most of the summer, playing a role in a big professional production of **A Midsummer Night's Dream**. He hadn't said that much about it, like not even mentioning any of the things Miss Scott had said about how famous the Mannsville **Shakespeare** Festival was, or why she thought he'd be a shoo-in for the part of Puck.

All he'd mentioned to Jancy was how he was marking off the days on the calendar until the school year was over and he'd be heading for Mannsville. But then Jancy had ducked her head and glanced at him out of the corner of her eye and said, "Yeah. Well, I guess I ought to think it's swell that you're going to be away all summer being a famous actor and not having to worry about"—long pause—"anything."

But when he'd asked her what she meant, she'd only shrugged and turned her head away, so that her face was hidden behind a thick curtain of curly hair. Jancy did that a lot when she didn't want you to know what she was thinking.

He should have known better than to press his luck, but he could see there was some sort of problem, and he really wanted to know what it was.

So he asked her right out, "Gee whiz, Jancy. Tell me. What's the matter?"

"What do you mean?" Jancy said, turning away to put a stack of plates in the cupboard. "Nothing's the matter. Not a thing." That was exactly *what* she said, word for word, but the *way* she said it made it mean exactly the opposite.

Afterward, when William had time to give it some more thought, he still didn't get it. He was pretty sure it wasn't simply that Jancy was jealous of his good luck.

Jancy always had her own way of making decisions, and once they were made she really stuck to them, but she'd never been jealous of good things that happened to other people. At least not William and the little kids. She'd always seemed to be really happy when any of them, Trixie or Buddy or William himself, got to do, or have, something special.

Take for instance, just a few days ago, when the *Gold Beach News* did a story about the extra-large first-grade class, and Trixie got to have her picture in the paper. The photographer from the *News* had looked around the jam-packed first-grade class at Gold Beach Elementary, and then picked Trixie, out of all those kids, to come up and stand beside the blackboard and point to where her teacher had written every first grader's name. All thirty-three of them.

Jancy had seemed to be happy about that, even when Trixie cut out the picture and kept insisting that everybody admire it, over and over again. "Don't I look famous?" she kept saying. "People who get their picture in the paper are famous, aren't they?" It didn't take long for Buddy to get fed up and say he was going to look a lot famouser when he was in first grade. But Jancy went on patiently looking at the picture and agreeing that Trixie looked pretty famous.

It wasn't just jealousy, William was pretty sure of that. So what was Jancy fretting about? Of course there were always the Baggetts, but he'd asked her more than once if she was still worrying about them showing up again, and she'd said no. What she'd actually said was, "Not really. I mean, they can't take us back again. I mean not legally. Legally none of us are Baggetts anymore, *but . . .*" She'd shrugged and sighed and stopped talking. William got the picture. You could get your name changed, and move a hundred miles away, but that didn't mean you could get the Baggetts out of your bloodstream, not to mention your nightmares. Particularly your nightmares.

William had gotten that far wondering about what ailed Jancy, when he reached the post office and got in the line of people waiting to mail or pick up packages. The line wasn't that long, only three or four people, but the person at the head of it was a kid who was in William's gym class at Gold Beach Junior High. A kid named Charlie something, who was at the moment grinning at William and giving him a fairly friendly "Hi."

But after William returned the "Hi," the other kid turned around and picked up his package and left, without stopping to say anything more, leaving William to wonder if his "Hi" had been too friendly, or something. Like maybe he wanted too much to be a different kind of person. Not necessarily the most popular kind, but just someone that everybody knew and liked.

Of course it had been a lot better starting school here in Gold Beach, where he was just another new kid, and not "one of those good-for-nothing Baggetts." Which was the reaction he used to get, even after he'd more or less starred in Miss Scott's production of 𝕿𝖍𝖊 𝕿𝖊𝖒𝖕𝖊𝖘𝖙. Being a Hardison in Gold Beach was a big improvement over being a Baggett in Crownfield, even a Baggett who'd done pretty well in a school play.

And then it was his turn at the counter, and the clerk asked his name and handed him a big box. A really big box, carefully wrapped in brown paper and tied with lots of string. His name and address were printed on it very neatly, and the post office stamp said Crownfield, but there wasn't any return address. For a moment he considered opening it immediately, but then, supposing it might be something kind of personal, he wrapped his arms around it and took off, heading for the grocery store, and then on home to 971 Eleanor Street.

CHAPTER

2

Planning to open his mysterious package in the privacy of his room, William went around to the back door and entered as quietly as possible. Why? No particular reason, except that a person who'd just received a large box and hadn't the slightest idea who might have sent it just might need to get used to whatever it turned out to be before he had to explain it to other people. That's what he was thinking, anyway, as he snuck across the kitchen.

But he didn't make it. He had managed to put the bag of groceries down on the counter, and had gone only a few silent steps across the room when a familiar voice said, "Hi, William. What's in the box?" When he looked around, no one was there.

It was a voice he recognized, though. Saying "Trixie?" he looked some more. Then he knew; knew even before she stuck her curly head and baby-doll face out from under the kitchen table. Trixie liked to do something she called "Secret Places," which in her case seemed to mean finding a place she could hide. She really liked it best when she could drape a sheet over a piece of furniture and crawl under it. But when she didn't have a sheet, she made do with anything she could get under or behind.

Actually, Jancy—and William, too—had worried some about Trixie and her hiding places. About how it was somehow related to the way she used to try to keep herself hidden away when they were back at the Baggetts' and Big Ed had made her watch while he beat William with his belt. But Aunt Fiona thought it was best just to let her alone and she'd probably grow out of it.

And now, here she was scooting out from under the table and asking, way too loudly, about the box. "What's in the box, William?" she squealed. Of course, that did it. In less than a minute the rest of them were there too. So all three of them—Jancy and Buddy as well as Trixie— were crowding around and watching his every move, as he got out Aunt Fiona's kitchen scissors and started cutting string; cutting lots of tough string. When the box was finally open, William reached in and took out a lot of wadded-up *Crownfield Daily* newspapers—several big handfuls. Lots of *Dailys* and then, finally, another smaller box wrapped in fancy "Happy Birthday" paper and tied with a blue ribbon.

"Oh look," Trixie squealed. "It's a present. What is it, William? Who gave it to you?"

Then Buddy asked the same thing. "Who gave it to you, Willum? Was it Santa Claus?"

"No, dummy," Trixie said. "Santa Claus doesn't give birthday presents. That's a birthday present. See? It says so. Right there." Actually, Trixie, who was just starting first grade, couldn't read that much yet, but the wrapping paper had lots of pictures of cakes with candles on them. So you didn't have to read all that well to figure out that the two fancy-looking words written under each cake were "Happy Birthday."

And then Jancy, who hadn't said anything before, gave William a sideways grin and said, "I bet I know who sent it."

Ignoring her, William slipped the ribbon off and carefully unwrapped the box. He lifted the cover and discovered—a loose-leaf binder. Well, not an ordinary canvas-covered one. The cover of this binder was made of very expensive-looking leather, smooth and slick on each side with a panel of fancy bumps down the center that looked like the hide of an alligator or maybe a crocodile. An expensive-looking loose-leaf notebook that could be buckled shut so it was almost like a briefcase. The kind of briefcase that lawyers might carry around to hold stuff about all their courtroom cases. Lawyers like Clarice's parents, for instance—a possibility that popped into his mind before it occurred to him that he'd rather not go in that direction.

But apparently Jancy already had. She was smiling at him, the kind of teasing grin she always used when she was about to say something about Clarice. So he didn't give her the chance. Quickly picking up his fancy binder, he headed for his room without even stopping long enough to settle the loud argument—loud and getting louder—between Trixie and Buddy about which one of them was going to get to play with the great big box. Trixie wanted it for a dollhouse, and Buddy was yelling something about a hangar for his airplanes. William kept going. Jancy could settle it. She was better at that sort of thing than he was.

Safely in his room, he sat down on his bed for a while, thinking and running his fingers over the rich, bumpy surface of the mysterious gift and even holding it to his nose to breathe in its expensive, leathery smell. But what to do with it?

At first he did consider getting out the faded and slightly scruffy loose-leaf binder that he'd been using at school, taking out all his notes and math papers, and putting them into . . . But then he thought again.

Nobody else at Gold Beach Junior High had a fancy alligator leather binder that looked like a briefcase. Or if they did, he certainly hadn't seen it. So there were going to be questions. And if he said it was a present, they might want to know who from—and even why. So William thought some more.

And that's pretty much how he happened to decide that his mysterious gift was just the thing he needed—for a new secret journal! A new one, because the one he'd started in the seventh grade, and had written in almost every night for a while, had completely disappeared. Somewhere in all the spur-of-the-moment moves—from the Baggetts' falling-down farmhouse, to the Ogdens' cellar, to Aunt Fiona's the first time, back to the Baggetts', and finally back again to Aunt Fiona's—the journal he'd been writing in for almost a year had turned up missing. Which was too bad, because there had been some pretty good stuff in it. The kind of stuff that, as Miss Scott suggested, told how you felt about the important things that happened to you, with sections where you put those happenings "on scene," where you included dialogue—what you'd said to someone, and what they'd answered back. Or in William's case, what he'd liked to have said if he'd had the nerve. Things like, "That's my book, Andy, and if you throw it, someday you're going to be *very, very sorry.*"

He could remember exactly when he'd written that one. It had been the day that Andy, one of the Baggett twins, had grabbed his new math book as he was going down the aisle in the school bus, and then all the way home kept threatening to throw it out of the window. And whenever William reached for it, Al, the other twin, punched him in the ribs or twisted his arm. Actually, Andy finally did throw the book, but by then they were nearly home and William had been able to find it lying there beside the road, only a little bit ragged and dirty. And that night, after he'd found the book, he went back and climbed up into his attic hideout and wrote a dialogue and recited it several times even before he did his math homework.

After the part about Andy being *very, very sorry*, he'd gone on to write more. It had gone something like, "You may be too dumb to realize it, but there are different ways to throw things, and someday I'm going to be the one who gets to do the throwing."

After that he'd had Andy say something stupid like, "Duh! Whatcha talking about, kid?" He'd done a pretty good Andy Baggett imitation whenever he read that part. He'd always been good at impersonating movie stars like Jimmy Cagney and Edward G. Robinson, so Andy Baggett was a cinch.

It really was too bad that the old journal was gone. He'd like to read some of it again to remind himself how lucky he was, how lucky all four of them were, to be back at Aunt Fiona's. But thinking ahead to next summer and the chance that he might be playing the part of Puck in an important production of A Midsummer Night's Dream, it really did seem like a good time to start another personal and very private journal where he would, once again, record every important and dramatic event that happened in his life.

So that was decided, and William found a good hiding place at the back of his closet and stashed his fancy new journal away until he could come up with an hour or two of absolute privacy.

## CHAPTER
### 3

It took a while. Privacy wasn't too easy to come up with when you were part of a family that included a sister as good at mind reading as Jancy, and a brother as hard to get away from as Buddy. So it wasn't until two or three days later that William was able to find a quiet moment to get started on his secret journal. In fact, it was rather late on a Friday night when he finally sat down at his desk and began:

> I, William S. Hardison, am writing this on the first day of October, 1938, and as you can see, it's only the first page. So nothing has happened to me before this date? Not likely, since I've been living for thirteen long years, and an awful lot has already happened to me.

He stopped writing for a moment—long enough to grin ruefully and underline the word "<u>awful</u>."

*But as for the present? Right now? Today? Well in a way, it's a good time for starting over, because I am now a Hardison. A legal Hardison, after starting life as a Baggett. Which, let me tell you, is not a good way to start.*

*I don't intend to say very much about that part of my life in this journal, because it's over and done with. And because, where Baggetts are concerned—the less said, the better. Right?*

He stopped again, holding his pen over the place where the next word would be written—considering whether that was all he needed to say about all those years as a Baggett. But then it occurred to him that someday, when that whole miserable mess was a *long* way behind him—and he was, just maybe, a more or less important person—there might be some interest in what could be called his life story. That is, in finding out where he'd started, and how far he'd come. So the next paragraph began . . .

*However, a few words might be a good idea, just to set the stage.*

He rather liked that—the part about "setting the stage" particularly, since it was looking like the "stage" might turn out to be an important part of his life. He nodded approvingly and went on:

As I just said, I was born a Baggett, but my mother was Laura Hardison, Big Ed Baggett's second wife. His first wife, Mabel, had had four kids, one after the other just about as fast as physically possible, and as if that wasn't bad enough, two more at the same time—twins. I guess the twins must have been pretty scary even as newborns, because right after they arrived, Mabel gave up and ran away. No one seemed to know exactly what happened to her, but she never came back. So that was when my mother started taking care of the newborn twins, and for some reason she wound up getting married to Big Ed. So then I was born, and my sister Jancy, but by that time the other six Baggett kids were quite a bit older. And all six of them were way too big for their age. Not to mention, way too vicious.

Things weren't too bad for the first few years, while our mother was still around. But then, when I was about six years old Trixie was born, and two years later Buddy, and that was when my mother died.

After that things went from bad to worse—a lot worse—until the day when Al and Andy convinced Buddy that a toilet was a good place to give a guinea pig a whirlpool bath. Jancy isn't the type who flies off the handle, but having her only *pet, Sweetie Pie, flushed down the toilet turned out to be the last straw. I was sort of surprised when she decided we were going to run away— not someday in the future, but right now! Like tomorrow! And of course we had to take Trixie and Buddy with us.*

*The escape wasn't easy, and there were a couple of serious detours, but now we're living with our aunt, Fiona Hardison, in the town of Gold Beach, and next summer I'm probably going to be playing a part in a Shakespeare play. Not a school one this time, but a big-time professional production. And in the meantime I'm in the eighth grade at Gold Beach Junior High, and everything at school is a lot different from what it was in Crownfield.*

But enough about that, he told himself, as he put his secret journal back in its hiding place. Different, he was thinking. Yeah, in lots of ways. Not that he'd stop getting good grades. That had always been easy for him. But different from the kind of guy who was either ignored, or else teased and bullied, by all the other kids. Teased about being a teacher's pet in Miss Scott's classes, and made fun of for being the last one picked when teams were being chosen because he was so lousy at sports. But teased most of all about being a Baggett.

Most of that had already changed here at Gold Beach. The whole Baggett thing was behind him. There was no drama department, and no Miss Scott, which was too bad, but at least he wouldn't have the "teacher's pet" thing to worry about. There were still some problems, such as being small and scrawny for his age, and the fact that he was a total flop at sports.

Since getting enough healthy stuff to eat was a lot easier here at Aunt Fiona's, he was probably going to start catching up as far as size was concerned. But that still left the no-good-at-sports thing. He was working on that, too.

In the days that followed, the "lousy at sports" problem inspired a special page in the secret journal. On a page titled *Things to Practice*, William drew some columns where he planned to put down how much time he'd spent on practicing things such as *throwing, catching, batting*, and *running*. But the way it was turning out, the only column that grew very much was the *running* one. In the *running* column there were soon a lot of entries that said: *15 minutes running to school*, or *16 minutes running home from school*. But that was about it, since it turned out to be almost impossible to practice the other skills without someone to do it with.

He did manage to get in a little throwing practice by throwing a baseball at a spot on the trunk of the oak tree in Aunt Fiona's backyard. But having to run after the ball every time slowed things up considerably. And as for catching and batting—no entries at all, even after he got desperate enough to try to get Buddy to help him practice. He should have known better. Like everything Buddy did, he threw amazingly hard and fast for a four-year-old, but usually not anywhere near what he was aiming at. So—lots more running practice, but not much of anything else. He tried Jancy next, but she hated doing it, and her aim wasn't much better than Buddy's.

But then Mr. Gregory, the gym teacher, started teaching gymnastics. Mr. Gregory had specialized in gymnastics when he was in school, and after he'd talked to the school board about how healthy it was for kids to be limber and well balanced, he was allowed to teach gymnastics to the kids at Gold Beach Junior High every Tuesday and Thursday. And it turned out that while William wasn't anywhere near the strongest or toughest guy in his class, he was pretty close to being the most limber and acrobatic.

So William went from trying to practice throwing and catching, to working on some skills that seemed to come more naturally to him. He did things like cartwheels, backflips, rope shinnying, and handstands, not only in the gymnasium, but also in his own backyard. And before long in the old barn on the Bowens' farm, with Charlie Bowen, who was in his gym class and was turning into a kind of best friend. At least the kind of friend who likes to practice with you when you're doing some things you're both really good at.

The month of October crept slowly by, and then it was Halloween—which turned out to be a brand-new experience, not only for Trixie and Buddy but for William and Jancy, too. Oh, they knew about the kinds of things people did on Halloween, or at least they thought they did. They'd certainly heard the older Baggett kids bragging about the things they'd tipped over and smashed to pieces, and the people they'd scared to death. But since Halloween seemed to make Baggetts even more vicious than usual, William and Jancy had known better than to try to do anything when October 31 rolled around—except keep out of sight. So things like dressing up in costumes and neighborhood trick-or-treating were as new to them as they were to Trixie and Buddy.

The year went slowly on. Christmas was a completely new and wonderful experience for all four of the ex-Baggetts. There were presents that everybody bought or made for one another. And, of course, a Christmas tree, and caroling with some other kids in the neighborhood. The Christmas tree, decorated with ornaments and tinsel, was a special treat for all of them, since the only time the Baggetts ever had a tree was one year when Rudy and Little Ed stole a real big one from the town square. It had lost most of its ornaments, so it didn't look too good, but it did make the house smell a lot better than usual. But Big Ed knew the Baggetts were on the Crownfield police department's "usual suspects" list when anything disappeared downtown, so he burned it up in the fireplace after only a few hours. Which was too bad, but at least the house was a little warmer for a while.

Then came Easter, with special days at Aunt Fiona's church and lots of new clothes and egg hunts. All of which were things that, like Halloween and Christmas, were new experiences for the ex-Baggetts. Going to church at all was also different. William and Jancy might have gone more often, but with Aunt Fiona so awfully busy, and with Buddy making a pest of himself in Sunday school, they didn't get to go very often.

School, for William, was okay in most ways. As usual, he had no trouble making good grades and getting along with teachers. He still wasn't all that great at any sport that required a lot of height or big muscles, but he continued to be a natural at things like backflips and handstands and shinnying up ropes.

Later that spring it was Jancy who decided that Mother's Day should be celebrated by giving Aunt Fiona presents. Mostly those consisted of thinking up new ways to help with all the extra work she had to do because of suddenly having a houseful of kids. William and Jancy learned how to do laundry and ironing, and Buddy tried to get into the act—by digging all the holey socks out of Aunt Fiona's sewing basket and mending them with glue from William's model airplane kit. Another dumb kid disaster. Not quite as awful as flushing Sweetie Pie down the toilet, but nearly as bad. Aunt Fiona said Buddy meant well, even though about a dozen socks were pretty

much goners. But then Aunt Fiona tended to think that
way, where Buddy was concerned.

And of course, all year long there was 𝕬 𝕸idsummer
𝕹ight's 𝕯ream to look forward to—and practice for.
It wasn't long before his big ℭomplete 𝖂orks of 𝖂illiam
𝕾hakespeare just naturally fell open to that particular play
when he picked it up—pages 387 to 411—and he had all
of Puck's lines by heart. He'd memorized them so well
that he could not only recite them silently in bed at
night but also act them out now and then, for the rest
of the family. Sometimes his audience was just Jancy and
Pumpkin, her new guinea pig, but now and then he managed to get Trixie and Buddy to sit still for a scene or two.

On some days it seemed the year was flying by, but
now and then it felt, to William at least, that time was
standing still. He went on crossing out each day that
passed with a big dark X on his private calendar, and
writing down how many days were left until the middle
of June 1939, when he would leave for Mannsville
College, to be in 𝕬 𝕸idsummer 𝕹ight's 𝕯ream. But only
on his own private calendar, because, for some reason, it
upset Jancy when he used the one in the kitchen.

Sometimes he would get attacks of impatient frustra-
tion, in spite of the fact that in many ways it was the best
year of his life. But when that happened he got through
it by writing in his secret journal. Usually it was fairly late
at night when he would get his new leather-covered binder

from its secret hiding place at the back of his closet, climb into bed, and start writing. He would write things like:

Here I am again, and there's still a long time to wait until June. Yesterday my favorite teacher—at least my favorite one here in Gold Beach—assigned everyone to recite something from Shakespeare. How about that for a coincidence? And talk about easy! While the rest of the class was going to the library and trying to find something not too hard to memorize, all I had to do was say, and kind of act out, one of the speeches I've been practicing for six months. The one where Puck is talking to King Oberon and he says,

"Captain of our fairy band,
Helena is here at hand;
And the youth, mistook by me,
Pleading for a lover's fee.
Shall we their fond pageant see?
LORD, what fools these mortals be."

I think Mrs. Peters was kind of shocked when I threw up my hands and said LORD that way, but it _was_ Shakespeare, wasn't it? Anyway, the class liked it.

Living in Gold Beach with Aunt Fiona was turning out to be even better than William had ever imagined it could be. And most of the time, at least during the day, William managed to almost forget about what being a Baggett had been like. But sometimes in dreams, or even wide awake in the middle of a dark, still night, it all came back. Not in real, clear-cut scenes, but more like some kind of a ghost story where dark floating shadows would appear and only gradually begin to look and sound like something or someone from his Baggett-haunted past. And William would have to tell himself over and over again that it was over, done with, and the Baggetts were never coming after him again. And most of the time he believed it.

Finally it was June 1, and time to really begin making plans for the summer. William had been saving up money all year by doing odd jobs around the neighborhood. He wanted to have enough to pay for his bus ticket from Reedly to Crownfield, and to use for spending money, when he was too busy being a professional actor to get out and earn any. So he, once again, had a Getaway Fund something like the one he'd kept in his attic hideout back at the Baggetts'. Only this time it didn't have to be a carefully hidden secret.

At last the school year ended, William graduated from the eighth grade, and it was almost time to pack. Miss Scott had written to say that she would pick him up at the Crownfield bus station on June 16, and he could ride the rest of the way to Mannsville with her. He could hardly wait. Talking to Miss Scott on the trip would be great. He would tell her about how he'd already memorized all of Puck's speeches and figured out all kinds of acting business to do while he recited, like she'd had him do when he was Ariel. Maybe she'd even want him to recite for her.

So everything was okay except Jancy was still having gloomy spells, without ever being willing to level with William about it. It wasn't like her. Jancy had always come right out and told him what she thought, like when she decided it was time for them to run away, but now she was obviously worried about something she wouldn't talk about. When he came right out and asked her, she would only shrug and say, "Don't worry about it." But sometimes he did.

Two or three times when he tried to get her to talk about it, she just shook her head and walked off. Once he even grabbed her wrist so she couldn't get away, and said, "Gee, Jancy. I'll bet you're still worrying about the Baggetts showing up again. You know what? I am too, at least I still have nightmares about it. Is that it? Do you have nightmares too?"

All Jancy did was shake her head and say no. But then she shrugged and added, "Not exactly."

On the morning of June 16, William woke up before the alarm went off, jumped out of bed, dressed hurriedly, and carried his loaded suitcase downstairs. Very heavily loaded—what with all his clothes and shoes, as well as his journal and his five-pound copy of 𝕾𝖍𝖆𝖐𝖊𝖘𝖕𝖊𝖆𝖗𝖊'𝖘 𝕮𝖔𝖒𝖕𝖑𝖊𝖙𝖊 𝖂𝖔𝖗𝖐𝖘. Parking the suitcase near the back door, he had the table all set before Aunt Fiona appeared, looking tousled and half-awake. Smiling sleepily, she said, "I thought I heard someone down here. You might think something important was going to be happening today."

"You think so?" William grinned. "I don't see why. Don't I always beat everyone downstairs?" Which wasn't exactly true. He looked at his new wristwatch, the one that Aunt Fiona had given him for an eighth-grade graduation present. "Maybe I better go help Jancy with the little kids. Okay?" Without waiting for an answer, he raced up the stairs and seconds later was lifting a half-awake Buddy out of bed and walking him toward the bathroom.

Halfway there, Buddy shook him off. "Turn me loose," he said. "You don't suppose to push me to the baffroom anymore. I go all by myself now."

True enough. The days when William had to walk a dead-to-the-world Buddy to the bathroom, or risk an accident that would get them both slapped around, were long gone. And now, a soon-to-be-five Buddy was fiercely proud of the fact that he was no longer a bed wetter. So William let him go on alone and went back to the kitchen, where Jancy and Trixie soon joined them. It wasn't quite eight o'clock when they all piled into Aunt Fiona's old Dodge and were off to the bus stop in Reedly.

Actually, as William had tried to point out, it wasn't really necessary for them all to go. Trixie and Buddy, with Jancy there to keep an eye on them, would be fine for the short time it would take for Aunt Fiona to drive the few miles to the Reedly bus stop and back. But of course the little kids wanted to go, and it was Jancy who made sure it happened. She was the one who insisted that they all should get up early and go to Reedly to see William off on the Greyhound bus. William didn't see why, but what with Jancy being in such a touchy mood, he'd decided not to argue about it.

He did wonder why, though. Particularly that morning, when it became apparent that Jancy was in one of her strange glum-faced moods. But it wasn't until they reached the bus stop that William was able to pull her aside and ask her what was wrong. "You really don't know?" She shook her head and shrugged. "Maybe I'll write you about it," she said, and then, "Maybe I'll have to."

Meanwhile Trixie and Buddy were having a good time looking around and remembering how they had waited there for a ride to Gold Beach, almost a year before, when they were still runaways. A different man was at the desk, but when Trixie asked him if the man with the rumble seat still worked there, he said, "You must mean Joe Fisher. Sure, Joe still works here, but he's on the afternoon shift. And he still drives that old Model A now and then, when he can get it to run."

Trixie and Buddy were still chatting with the bus station guy, telling him how much they'd liked riding in the rumble seat, when the Greyhound bus pulled up to the curb. After a lot of hugging and kissing, William was off on his way to Crownfield, looking out the window to where Trixie and Buddy were jumping up and down and waving with both hands, and Jancy was standing there staring—glumly.

Just as it had before, the almost one-hundred-mile trip between Reedly and Crownfield seemed to take forever, but for a very different reason. A year ago it had been a tense and nerve-jangling ride for William and Jancy too. Back then they'd been running away to Aunt Fiona's, without knowing whether she would welcome them, or tell them to get out and get lost. And then too, there had been that guy on the bus whom William had recognized as one of Rudy Baggett's crummy gang, who probably would—and sure enough did—tell Big Ed where and when he'd seen them. So that long bus ride had been stretched out by tension and worry. But this time the long trip, with its lunch stop in Summerford, seemed to be taking forever simply because William was so eager and anxious for . . . well, you might say, for the show to begin. The show in which he was going to have the chance to be a real actor in a professional production that would last most of the summer and be seen by thousands of people.

The hours crawled by endlessly, but finally the bus lurched and shuddered into the station in downtown Crownfield, and, with his nose pressed to the window, William looked out and saw . . . not Miss Scott, but Clarice Ogden.

Quickly moving back out of sight, William told himself he should have expected it. After all, Miss Scott had written to say that Clarice was staying with her for the summer while her folks were away, so of course she, too, would be going to Mannsville. But for some reason it hadn't occurred to him that she might be riding down with them. And now, looking out of the bus window and seeing her standing there looking so familiar—and yet so strangely different—was startling. The difference surprised him most—how much she seemed to have changed in such a short time. After all, it was just last summer when she had hidden the runaway Baggetts in her basement.

Scrunching down to where he'd be harder to see from the sidewalk, he peeked out again. Her hair had changed, for one thing—now it was sleeked down and flipped up at the edges. And also her mouth. Bigger and a lot redder, too. Lipstick, maybe? But what else was new? Her shape, perhaps? Not that she hadn't had one when he knew her before. But it looked different now. In what way? The word that came to William's mind was "female."

William knew quite a lot about the whole sex thing. Anyone would who had grown up around a bunch of loudmouthed Baggetts, one of whose favorite topics of conversation, next to driving and drinking, was sexy stuff. But Baggett sex talk always seemed to be about "dames" or "babes"—or a few other terms, none of which he had ever connected with the Clarice he'd known back there in the Ogdens' basement. This Clarice was something else again, and it was kind of a shock. And then, when he'd managed to pull himself together and climb down off the bus, and she caught sight of him, there was an even more shocking moment, when it looked like she was going to throw her arms around him.

Almost, but not quite. After she'd rushed forward with her arms spread out—and stopped just in time— he managed to say, "Hey. I almost didn't recognize you."

And then added, stupidly, "You look—great. Uh—that is—I mean different."

He winced, realizing it sounded like he meant she hadn't looked great before, but fortunately, she didn't seem to take it that way. She stared at him rather coolly for a moment and then said, "You don't. Look different, I mean. At least not much."

To his growing embarrassment, she stood back and surveyed him even more thoroughly. "Maybe a little taller, but still skinny." Then she added, nodding, "That's good, I guess, for being Puck, anyway. Puck probably should look kind of"—long pause while she looked him up and down again—"kind of—not exactly human?" She grinned. "Yeah, that's you, I guess."

He was still trying to decide how to answer when Miss Scott appeared, in a plain gray dress that might seem like a housedress on someone else, but on her, managed to look kind of dramatic. Patting him on the shoulder, she said, "So here you are, William. So good to see my Ariel again."

"You too." William gulped, hoping his wide grin said only how glad he was to see her, without giving away how much of it was relief that she'd appeared just in time to keep him from saying something else stupid to Clarice.

Next came the problem of trying to cram his suitcase into the trunk of Miss Scott's shiny green Oldsmobile along with a whole lot of other suitcases, and giving up and putting it on the backseat. William had started to climb in beside his suitcase when Clarice patted the front seat beside where she was sitting and said, "Why don't you sit up here too? So we can talk."

But Miss Scott came to the rescue again. This time by saying, "Oh, I think not. It will be too hot in the valley to be comfortable with all of us packed into the front seat. We can hear William fine from back there." She gave him one of her special smiles. "As I recall, he knows how to project."

So the long trip to Mannsville started with William riding in the backseat alone, except for his suitcase, and waiting for Clarice to stop talking long enough for him to ask Miss Scott some important questions. Or at least "project" them in her direction, and hope Clarice would shut up long enough to let Miss Scott answer.

he trip from Crownfield to Mannsville took more than three hours, so there was a lot of time to talk. At least a lot of time for Clarice to talk, while William and Miss Scott did a lot of listening. Twisted around so that her chin rested on the back of the front seat, Clarice stared at William and said things like, "Why were you so surprised to see me at the bus stop, William? You sure looked surprised." Then, without waiting for an answer, "Didn't you know Julia would be taking us both to Mannsville today? You should have known. My folks left for Chicago last Wednesday, so I've already been staying with Julia for quite a while."

And then to Miss Scott, who seemed to be trying to get a word in edgewise, "Yes, yes. I know. I'll remember to call you Miss Scott when we get there, but William already knows my parents have known you forever, and I've always called you Julia."

She went on then for a long time about how she'd stayed with Julia before when her folks were traveling, and how she'd had to be quiet about that when she was in one of Julia's classes because the other kids might think she was getting special treatment. "So it won't be hard for me to remember to call you Miss Scott," Clarice went on. "The only hard part this year was packing—because of this whole Mannsville thing. Always before, if I forgot something we could just drive over to my house and get it, but we can't do that this year, so I had to be sure to remember to pack all sorts of important stuff." A brief pause while Clarice's eyes suddenly opened wide—and then narrowed to a sneaky slit. "Didn't you have to bring a lot of important stuff, William?"

Remembering all the suitcases in the trunk, William could believe that Clarice had brought "a lot of important stuff."

"What important stuff did you have to remember to bring?" Clarice was insisting.

"Nothing much," he managed and then took the opportunity to try to sneak in a question. "Miss Scott," he started, but once again Clarice interrupted. Rolling her eyes in a strange way, she repeated, "Really, didn't you have some special stuff to bring?" More eye rolls, and then, "I mean, I'll bet you had a lot of books and things like that to bring along? I mean, stuff like, well, like that big Shakespeare book of yours and—and maybe a binder to keep important notes in? Or maybe a journal?"

*So that's it,* William thought. He was beginning to guess what she was driving at.

Turning to Miss Scott, Clarice went on, "Did you know William's been writing a journal ever since you had us start one in seventh grade? I'll bet he's planning to write one this summer." She nodded slowly and significantly. "Especially this summer, I'll bet."

She paused long enough to send another meaningful eye flick in William's direction. He got the picture. The picture of a mysterious birthday present with nothing to tell who sent it. At the time he'd pretty much guessed, even though he'd tried not to. But now he knew for sure. And he also knew, or at least strongly suspected, that it wasn't the last time he was going to hear about it. Keeping his eyes wide open in an "I can't imagine what you're talking about" stare, he tried not to consider the fact that Clarice had guessed he would use the fancy new binder for a journal.

Telling himself that it didn't really matter whether she'd sent him the binder or not, he managed to change the subject by sneaking in one of the questions he'd been wanting to ask. The one about how come Mannsville College happened to have such an important 𝕾𝖍𝖆𝖐𝖊𝖘𝖕𝖊𝖆𝖗𝖊 festival.

"The festival has been held at Mannsville for at least twenty years, during the school's summer vacation," Miss Scott answered. "It's very well known. The college has a large auditorium, with a fine proscenium stage. People come from all over the state to see the plays. Quite often some of the principal roles are played by professional actors, even some quite famous ones."

"Oh really?" Clarice squealed. "I didn't know that. You mean, like real movie stars? That's so exciting. Even stars like Jimmy Stewart and Bette Davis? But don't they have to pay them tons of money?"

Miss Scott laughed. "More often it's people whose experience has been on the stage rather than in the movies. And of course the professionals do get paid. But every year a few of the minor roles are given to talented beginners who aren't paid, except for being allowed to stay in one of the campus dormitories and eat at the cafeteria. I guess the feeling is that such people are already greatly rewarded by having a chance to have a wonderful foot-in-the-door acting experience." Catching William's eye in the rearview mirror, Miss Scott smiled at him, as she went on, "To play even a small role in a Mannsville production is considered an important step on the way to a stage career."

"Oh really?" Clarice asked. "But what happens if William and I don't get roles? What happens to people who come to audition and don't get a part?"

William had worried about that. Leaning forward, he listened anxiously as Miss Scott answered. "Well, that could happen. Some people who come to audition don't get chosen for a role. But in your case, Clarice, since you're staying with me this summer and I'm on the staff, you'll be allowed to stay in one of the dorms, even if you don't get a part. People on the staff are allowed to bring dependents. In that case you probably could sign up to do some backstage work, if you want to.

"And as for you, William, right at first there may be people in your dorm who've come to audition, and will be leaving soon if they don't get a role. But I really don't think *you* have to worry. I'm to be involved in the auditions, and knowing your experience and ability as well as I do, I feel quite sure you'll get the part of Puck."

"Will other people be trying out for Puck?" William asked.

"I think two others have signed up to audition for the role," Miss Scott said. "But from what I hear, they won't be much competition."

That was a relief. Leaning back in the seat, William shut his eyes and let his imagination bring up exciting, slightly scary scenes of what it might be like, auditioning for a part in a real theater. He pictured himself on an empty stage reciting lines, while a whole bunch of important-looking people watched him closely and wrote things in notebooks. It was a scene he'd imagined before but not in such a vivid and immediate way. It was scary, all right, but it did help to remember how, when he started acting the role of Ariel, he'd been scared at first, but then he'd learned how to forget who he really was. How he'd been able to forget that a Willy Baggett had ever existed, and just let the personality of magical Ariel take over.

It was a memory that did conjure up a little bit of confidence. A hope that Puck might just do the same thing. He did have reason to think that might happen, because it already had now and then, when he had been saying his 𝔐idsummer 𝔑ight's lines for Aunt Fiona and the kids. He'd say a line like, "'𝔗hou speak'st aright. /𝔍 am that merry wanderer of the night,'" and the words seemed to say themselves, and come out in a cocky, self-confident way. In the way that a "hobgoblin" called Puck, or sometimes, Robin Goodfellow, would have said them.

He was still concentrating on that memory when something told him to open his eyes, and when he did it was to see that Clarice had once again twisted around and was staring at him with her chin on the back of the seat. "Well, hi," she said. "You were sleeping, weren't you?" Her smile was teasing. "He was sleeping, Julia, like a baby. Isn't that cute?"

"No I wasn't," he told her indignantly. "I was just thinking."

She giggled. "Yes, he was. He was sleeping."

But then a slightly Puckish feeling oozed up, and William grinned and said, "Well, actually, what I was doing was acting. I was being Demetrius in act three. You know, where it says Demetrius **'lies down and sleeps.'** Pretty good acting, don't you think?"

Miss Scott laughed and said, "Very convincing. I'm impressed."

Clarice stared at Miss Scott and then at William, frowned, flounced around, and stopped talking, at least for the time being.

## CHAPTER 7

s the trip went on, the time began to pass more quickly because . . . well, probably because Clarice had stopped talking and there was so much to think and wonder and worry about. And so it was, for William at least, something of a surprise when the Oldsmobile slowed down to turn off onto a tree-lined road. Pressing his nose to the window, William watched eagerly as some large buildings came into view. Big, important-looking stone buildings sitting on green lawns under tall, shady trees. Somehow it looked almost too perfect to be real. Just the right dramatic sort of place for a Shakespeare festival to be held.

When the car came to a stop, it was in front of a large building where, above wide double doors, there was a permanent engraved sign that said EDWIN HALL. And under that a smaller hand-printed one that said SHAKESPEARE FESTIVAL CAST HOUSING. PLEASE REGISTER AT THE OFFICE ON YOUR RIGHT.

Right at that moment all of it—all the memorizing

and practicing and daydreaming—came down to an immediate, insistent reality. Came down to walking into a huge, official-looking building to register as a real actor who was here to audition for an important part in a 𝔖hakespeare play.

"This is it," Miss Scott was saying. "Here's where you'll be staying, William," and he was getting out of the car and staring up at the big entryway and thinking . . . No, not thinking as much as feeling . . . Feeling like getting back in the car and telling Miss Scott that he—that both of them—had made a big mistake. That he didn't know why they'd ever thought that a scrawny, undersized kid who'd been born into the good-for-nothing Baggett family could walk into a big, beautiful building with a bunch of people who really were experienced actors, and pretend he belonged there.

But then Miss Scott was standing beside him with her hand on his shoulder and telling Clarice, "Wait here. I'll be back as soon as William gets registered." The rest turned out to be quick, if not easy. Walking into a large, nicely furnished lounge area, they approached a desk at which a receptionist, an official-looking gray-haired lady, was waiting to sign him in. After he'd answered a few questions and signed his name, he was given a key and told to take the stairs to his left and he would find his room—217—on the floor above.

So that's what he did. Acting—and it really was just

acting—as if everything was okay, as if he knew exactly what he was doing and why, he listened while Miss Scott told him she'd be back to take him to dinner at six o'clock, told her good-bye, and started up the stairs. And when she called after him to ask if he needed help with his suitcase, he called back, "No, I'm fine. Everything's fine," and managed to sound like he meant it. But it was all an act, and he knew it.

He had to keep acting when he got upstairs and passed someone in the hall. Walked right past a tall man with a handsome movie-star-type face. Obviously an actor—a real one. A man who nodded and said hello. And William nodded back and went on down the hall until he came to room 217, where he unlocked the door, went in, put down his suitcase, sat down on it, and stared into space.

Right at first he was barely aware of his surroundings. He was so busy thinking about the mess he was in that he noticed only slowly that the room was furnished in a comfortable businesslike way with a bed, a dresser with a big mirror, a desk with nothing on it except a dictionary and a book of photographs of Mannsville College, and some pictures on the walls. When he'd talked to the woman at the desk and then again, when he'd met the tall actor in the hall, what he had been doing, of course, was playing a part. The part of an experienced actor who was there because he was going to have a role in Mannsville

College's **Shakespeare** festival production. He must have done it well enough, he decided, to have fooled the woman at the desk, as well as the guy in the second-floor hall. Had fooled them into thinking that the person they were speaking to was someone who had the right to be there. Had they really been fooled? he wondered. Or had they seen right through him and were just being polite until he was out of sight, when they would start laughing, or even call the police to come throw him out?

He'd been sitting there for several minutes before it occurred to him that there might be another way to look at the problem. The other way might be that it didn't matter if down underneath he was still an undersized, thirteen-year-old ex-Baggett. What mattered right now was how quickly he could learn to play the all-day, every-day role of William **S**. Hardison, self-confident, sophisticated guy, who was there at the Mannsville **Shakespeare** Festival for the very good reason that he was an experienced actor who would be playing the important role of Puck.

He looked at his watch. Four thirty, which meant that he had about an hour and a half before Miss Scott came back to take him to dinner. Not much time. He stood up, squared his shoulders, took a deep breath, and got to work playing the part of a self-confident, experienced actor, busily and efficiently unpacking his suitcase, and feeling right at home in a huge fancy building where only actors were going to be allowed to live.

As usual, making up a role and acting it out came naturally to William. As he unpacked, he was doing a relaxed, almost bored, character. Maybe that of a well-known actor arriving from a stint on the Broadway stage, unpacking his fancy suits and expensive tuxedo, and getting ready to go out on the town.

Actually, it didn't take all that long to get his meager wardrobe unpacked: one extra pair of pants, three short-sleeved shirts, and some socks and underpants. And at five minutes to six, still hanging on to his cool, sophisticated role, he nodded calmly to the receptionist on his way out to sit on the front steps of Edwin Hall and wait for Miss Scott to arrive.

## CHAPTER 8

That night at dinner William pretty much managed to hold on to his cool, sophisticated role, while discussing the Mannsville campus with Miss Scott and Clarice. At times he almost convinced himself. But not completely. Now and then he was uneasily aware of the fact that, down underneath the calm and collected role he was playing, the same old natural-born Willy Baggett was lying in wait for a chance to take over and trip him up.

The restaurant was an Italian one in downtown Mannsville, and the food was great, but William was almost too busy staying in character to notice. They were eating there, Miss Scott explained, because the Shakespeare festival cafeteria hadn't opened yet. "But starting tomorrow," she told William, "you'll eat your meals there."

She got out a map of the campus, gave it to William, and pointed out Edwin Hall and the path that led to the cafeteria. "It's not far," she said, "so you can run down there and have something to eat whenever it fits into your schedule. You'll just have to show your cast member card as you go in, at least at first, until they get to know you. Oh yes, and tomorrow morning the auditions will start at nine, and yours isn't scheduled until quite a bit later, so you won't need to have an early breakfast. But just to be sure, be here, at the auditorium"—she pointed out an impressively large square on the map—"by a little before ten."

As he opened his mouth to say he'd be there it hit him again. The feeling that this whole talented-actor thing was some kind of crazy daydream, and that any moment he was going to stop dreaming and be so terrified he couldn't even breathe, let alone recite a whole bunch of Shakespeare. No telling what he might have said or done, except right at that moment Clarice pushed her face, with its shiny red lips and stylish hairdo, close to his and asked, "Do you think you can find your way to the auditorium? I could come over tomorrow morning and show you the way."

Somehow the way she said it got to him. Gulping down the rising tide of panic, William pulled himself back into his act and said, with a calm smile, "Thanks, but no thanks." And then, even more coolly, "I'm pretty good at reading maps."

It wasn't until later that night, when he was back in his room in Edwin Hall, that William had enough time and privacy to really examine what had happened, and almost happened, to him since he arrived at Mannsville. The first thing he did was open the window and lean out, thinking that maybe the cool, quiet evening air would help him to feel more calm and confident. But leaning out and looking at the beautifully landscaped grounds with all the towering trees and smooth sweeps of lawn only seemed to emphasize how hard it was for a Baggett, even an ex-Baggett, to feel at home in such a place. It wasn't until then that it occurred to him that, once again, it might help to understand how he was feeling if he put some of his thoughts and emotions down in pen and ink.

Getting out the alligator binder and flipping to the first blank page, he sat down at the desk, just sat there for a while running his fingers over the little leathery ridges and breathing in the expensive leathery smell.

Which, of course, brought back the things Clarice had said in the car that made it impossible for him to go on pretending that he didn't know who had sent it to him. It had been Clarice, he knew that now, even though he still wasn't sure why. Or why she *now* wanted to be certain that he knew she was the one who'd done it. Why was that? There was, of course, the unlikely possibility that Jancy had known what she was talking about when she brought up that being-in-love stuff. That the journal was some kind of a very personal gift, like flowers or even maybe a ring. But on the other hand, it might just be that Clarice wanted him to know that he owed her one.

That, he decided, was more likely. He had no idea just exactly how she would want him to pay her back, but he had a feeling it wouldn't be long until he found out.

He sighed, shook his head, and turned his attention back to the more urgent problem—the one that he had really meant to write about. Fishing his pen out of his pocket, he stared at the blank page for a long time before he began to write.

> *Well, here he is. Here's the skinny little guy who used to be the Baggett gang's favorite punching bag, and now he's actually writing this in a big ancient Greek-style building called Edwin Hall, surrounded by acres of green lawns and lots of huge trees, where he's supposed to live all summer. In the same building where a bunch of honest-to-God stage actors from places like Broadway or Hollywood are going to be moving in tomorrow morning.*

After reading over what he'd written, he shook his head again, started to cross it all out, and decided it wasn't worth the effort. But when he started a new paragraph, it was back in first person.

*And also tomorrow morning (TOMORROW as in the very next day of my life) I'm going to have to audition for the part of Puck in A Midsummer Night's Dream. And the problem is, most of the time I'm scared to death.*

*The only time that I'm not is when I'm doing such a good job of acting cool and collected that for a minute or two I almost convince myself.*

He stopped writing, read over what he'd written, and decided that pretty much said it. But what good did that do? What good was being able to describe the problem, when describing it didn't necessarily solve anything? According to Miss Scott's theory, once you'd organized a problem well enough to be able to write about it, the solution was supposed to pop up like a jack-in-the-box. In this case, the solution to the terrifying fact that when he allowed himself to think about what was going to happen tomorrow morning, he could barely remember his own name, let alone all the things Puck was supposed to say and do.

Puck's speeches—but which ones? Miss Scott had told him that at the audition, she and probably two other casting people, including Mr. Andre, the executive director, would ask him to present a Puck speech of his own choosing. And after that he would be expected to respond to a reader who would read a cue to any one of

Puck's scenes, and he'd have to take it from there.

A speech of his own choosing, he thought. That ought to be easy. Like maybe . . . Without even opening 𝕿𝖍𝖊 𝕮𝖔𝖒𝖕𝖑𝖊𝖙𝖊 𝖂𝖔𝖗𝖐𝖘, he picked up his pen and began to write.

*"Through the forest have I gone,"*

He went on writing clear down to:

*"For I must now to Oberon."*

So he hadn't forgotten. Not any of the words he had to say in that scene. And he also remembered a lot of what actors called "business." Things he'd thought up to do while he was saying the words, and then practiced over and over again in front of Jancy and sometimes the kids and Aunt Fiona. How he'd stomped and strutted around, pretending to be looking for someone, before he stopped and started the speech. And how surprised he'd acted when he found Lysander and then Hermia, and the big deal he'd made of sprinkling the juice from the magic flower on Lysander's eyes.

*It's all still there in my head,* he wrote. And then underlined the words, pressing down so hard that the line was deep and dark. *It's all still there. So what am I afraid of?*

Several minutes later, after starting to write, and then stopping, and then starting again, he finally scribbled . . .

> *I keep telling myself to remember that back at Crownfield High, I was scared <u>every</u> time before I went onstage. But then Ariel would just sort of take over, and it was easy, and even fun. So why can't I believe that the same thing will happen when I go out on this stage?*

Right then, when he wrote the word *stage*, he began to remember something. What he suddenly knew was how and when he'd started to lose it. It all began when Miss Scott had been describing Mannsville College and had mentioned the huge theater and its especially grand proscenium stage. "Proscenium" was not a word that William had heard before, so of course he began to imagine what it might mean. Almost immediately, what he'd started picturing was something strange and foreign-looking—a vast, barren expanse, floating above a sea of frowning faces and staring eyes.

"Proscenium," he said, and then, questioningly, "Proscenium?" Putting down his pen, he closed his journal and reached for the *Webster's Dictionary*. And a half minute later he knew that a proscenium was simply the part of the stage between the curtain and the audience. And a proscenium stage was one that had a rounded or arched front to it. Pretty much like the one at Crownfield High School, only bigger, he supposed. No big deal.

He didn't know why it helped to know what the word meant, but it seemed to. Perhaps it was just because "proscenium" was obviously a word that a person who was planning on an acting career ought to know—and now he knew it. Or else it was because he knew now that he'd already been on a proscenium stage, and he'd done okay.

Not just okay, actually. Reminding himself of the article in the *Crownfield Daily* that said that the kid who played Ariel had been the hit of the show helped a little more. As he put his pen and journal away and crawled into bed, William was beginning to feel a little less terrified. He even slept—a little.

Morning finally came, and William was able to get dressed calmly enough, locate the map Miss Scott had given him, and find his way to the cafeteria, by not allowing his mind to go any further ahead than the next few seconds. Afterward he seemed to remember some scrambled eggs, but not much else. But whatever he'd eaten, when it was gone he only let his thinking move far enough along to get the map out of his pocket and use it to find the path that led to the auditorium.

On the way he forced himself to keep busy noticing things like the weather—warm and clear, but not really hot—and how the path cut across green lawns and passed groves of trees too perfect to be real. But then the narrow sidewalk came to an end at a wide street, and there, right up ahead, was a huge building with windowless walls, and at the end of a broad flight of stairs, a row of arched entryways.

Taking a deep breath and making a desperate try for a feeling of cool self-confidence, William started to climb up toward a small group of people who were standing near the entrance. All of them were strangers, except for one whom he recognized as the good-looking guy he'd seen in Edwin Hall. A man who, when he noticed William, said with a sarcastic grin, "Well, hello again, fellow thespian. You ready to face the Inquisition?"

When William asked, "Inquisition?" the man laughed and said, "Well, actually, just three tough casting directors." He pointed as he added, "The stage door is around the building to your right. Break a leg, kid."

That helped—a little. William didn't know why, except for the fact that he did know what actors meant when they told each other to "break a leg." Which was a reminder that he wasn't a complete beginner. He managed a thank-you and headed in the direction the man had pointed. Then came a long, lonely walk across the front of the huge building and down the other side to an official-looking back door, with a sign that said AUDITIONS 9:00 A.M. TO 2:30 P.M. William came to a stop, and then quickly, before he could chicken out, pushed open the door.

Inside the heavy door, a few steps led up to a dimly lit landing. A gray-haired man sitting behind a desk looked up and, by crooking a finger, summoned William to approach. He did, and when the man asked his name, he was barely able to whisper stiffly, "William Hardison."

"Okay. Let me check." The man ran his finger down a

page, came to a stop, and said, "Here you are." He looked at his watch and added, "You've come at a good time. Go on in and see if the previous young gentleman has finished. When he does, just walk out far enough to let the casting people see that you're here, and *raring to go*." His grin was sympathetic, but at the same time a little bit amused. Like he thought there was something funny about sending scared-to-death people out to face up to whatever it was that they'd foolishly imagined they were going to be able to do.

William managed to twitch his lips upward in a sorry imitation of a smile, before he turned toward a cavernous area divided by clumps of hanging curtains and sets. A place that looked a lot like backstage in the high school auditorium in Crownfield, only much wider, and higher, and more intimidating.

And then he was onstage. On the stage, and moving out toward what he now knew was the proscenium. A proscenium from which he could see an enormous expanse of empty seats and, farther back, two large balconies rising up toward a high domed ceiling. All of it empty except for the first row, where three people were looking up at him, an important-looking man with a little white beard and two women. One of the women was Miss Scott.

Somehow looking down at Miss Scott's smiling face only made it a whole lot worse. Worse because she was going to be sorry for him, and terribly embarrassed, since she'd probably told the other audition people how good he was going to be.

And then Miss Scott said something to the other two, turned, and raised her voice to say, "And so, William. What have you chosen to do for us today?"

He swallowed, swallowed again, and finally squeaked out, "Act two, scene two, where Puck is looking for Demetrius." Miss Scott and the others nodded, but their faces seemed to be reflecting the same walking-dead kind of rigidity that he was feeling as he turned away and made his way to the wings. Where he stopped, turned again, caught his breath, entered stage right, reached for—and became—Puck.

Moving forward on tiptoe, he could feel Puck's gleeful, roguish disposition curl his lips and flash from his eyes as he pranced and paused, looking from side to side—and then skipped forward again, searching here and there, peeking under imaginary bushes and pushing aside hanging branches as he hunted everywhere for the hard-hearted Athenian who was so scornful of the young woman who was madly in love with him. And whom Oberon, the king of the fairies, had sent Puck to find—and sprinkle with the love nectar from the magical flower.

When William/Puck reached midstage he stopped and shrugged, and speaking as if to himself, but at the same time, loud enough to be heard by an audience, he began to complain peevishly:

> "'Through the forest have J gone,
> But Athenian found J none,
> On whose eyes J might approve
> This flower's force in stirring love.'"

When he said, **"this flower,"** he held up an imaginary bell-shaped flower that he could almost see, right there in his hand. Turning it from side to side, he smiled, admiring its beauty. Then he moved on, still searching but less hopefully now, until he stopped to stare, startled by something he'd come on so suddenly he could hardly believe his eyes.

> "'Night and silence! Who is here?'"

He circled the sleeping Lysander, checking him out carefully before he went on:

> "'Weeds of Athens he doth wear:
> This is he, my master said,
> Despised the Athenian maid;'"

He tiptoed on until he found a sleeping maiden, and then bent solicitously over her and continued,

> "'And here the maiden, sleeping sound,
> On the dank and dirty ground.
> Pretty soul! she durst not lie
> Near this lack-love, this kill-courtesy.'"

Moving back to where he had left Lysander, he bent over and carefully sprinkled the flower's magic dew on one of his eyes and then the other, as he exclaimed,

> "'Churl, upon thy eyes I throw
> All the power this charm doth owe;
> When thou wak'st, let love forbid
> Sleep his seat on thy eyelid:'"

Circling around Lysander and then, once more, the sleeping maiden, he stepped back and held out both arms and cried,

> "'So awake when I am gone;
> For I must now to Oberon.'"

And then as he headed toward stage right, something, some bit of Puckishness, or perhaps just relief that he'd gotten through it, made him throw in a backflip followed by a brief handstand. Back on the proscenium, William smiled down at Miss Scott and the others, and the smile was still a Puckish one, and when the bearded man said,

"All right, young man. And now we're in act three, scene two, and your cue is Helena saying:

> "'And sleep, that sometimes shuts up sorrow's eye,
> Steal me awhile from mine own company.'

"And the stage direction says Helena 'lies down and sleeps.'"

And William/Puck/Robin Goodfellow, with barely a pause, recited and did the business he had planned and practiced all winter, pointing out three sleeping bodies, as he silently counted. One. He moved on to count two. And then three:

> "'Yet but three? Come one more;
> Two of both kinds make up four.'"

He reacted to Hermia's entrance with surprise and then compassion, before he went on:

> "'Here she comes, curst and sad:
> Cupid is a knavish lad,
> Thus to make poor females mad.'"

And when that was done, Miss Scott told him the audition was finished, and he would have known by the way she smiled at him, even if Puck hadn't already told him, that the part was his.

It wasn't Puck anymore, but it was a much more relaxed William than the one who had crept in, who stopped for a friendly chat with the man at the stage-door desk, before he went down the steps, and out into an astonishingly bright and beautiful mid-summer day.

As he walked, pranced almost, around the corner of the building, he was expecting to see the same group of people who'd been standing near the entrance. Looked forward to really seeing them, now that he no longer felt like a pitiful impostor about to be exposed as a fake. When he rounded the corner, they weren't there. But somebody else was.

Another kid, probably not much older than William himself, but taller and heavier, with a lot of slicked-back hair, broad shoulders, and a determined-looking chin, who was standing near the entrance of the theater. Standing there all by himself, but glancing around as if he were looking for someone. As soon as he noticed William, he came toward him.

"Hey kid," he was saying. "Did you just audition?"

William nodded, standing his ground, but not rushing into anything. Even though some of the Puckish self-confidence was still with him, it wasn't quite enough to overcome so many years of having been at the bottom of a top-heavy teenage pecking order. When the big kid finished sauntering over to stand only a couple of feet away, he shrugged and said, "You were trying out for Puck. Right?"

William nodded yes, before a bit of remaining Puckishness gave him the nerve to add, "How about you?"

The big kid grinned. "Yeah," he said, "I did. I'm Bernard. Bernard Olson?" in a tone of voice that clearly meant that he expected William to say something like, "Oh really? You're Bernard Olson himself? Gee! I'm so impressed!"

Since he'd never heard of Bernard Olson, all William said was, "Yeah?" But in a tone of voice that must have made it sound like, "And who is Bernard Olson?" because the Bernard person went on to explain impatiently.

"My dad is Professor Olson. You know, Dean of Performing Arts."

"Yeah?" William said in the same "so what" tone of voice.

"Yeah," the Bernard kid said with a shrug that said he was about to give up on William, but he obviously wasn't quite ready to.

"So," he went on, "how did it go?" He nodded toward the theater. "In there."

William grinned. "Pretty good, I guess."

Bernard shrugged again. He seemed to have quite a repertoire of shrugs. "Good for you. But if I were you, I wouldn't count on it."

"Oh? Why's that?" William asked.

"Well"—another shrug—"my dad talked me into auditioning. He helped me rehearse, and he thinks I'm pretty sure to get the part."

It was then that something, maybe that long-lasting shred of Puckishness, made William grin and say, "I wouldn't count on it."

une 17, 1939

Wow! What a day! I went off this morning so scared I really came close to running out to the highway and hitchhiking to wherever the first car that came along happened to be going, as long as it was so far away they'd never find me. What I was so scared of was that I was going to go out on the stage and really blow it and embarrass Miss Scott to death, not to mention myself. But then, somehow, when I walked out there onto the ~~procinium, prosenium~~

Scratching out a couple of tries, he opened the dictionary, reminded himself of the spelling, and went on:

when I walked out onto the proscenium, it was all right there after all—just like it used to be when I was in <u>The Tempest.</u> Maybe even more so. I wasn't scared anymore, but it wasn't because

*I knew how well I was doing. I was just Puck looking all over the forest for a guy dressed like an Athenian because Oberon, king of the fairies, told me I had to. Looking, getting bored with looking, sitting down and pouting for a few seconds, then getting up and finding what I was looking for. And then getting a kick out of playing a trick on a guy who'd been giving a poor lonesome maiden a hard time.*

*And when I got back here to Edwin Hall, there was a phone message waiting for me that said I had the part and I could pick up my member-of-the-cast ID card the next time I went to the greenroom. Wow! Wow! Wow!*

Getting up from the desk, William threw himself on his bed and just lay there grinning. After a while he started remembering how he'd run into that kid named Bernard, who had auditioned for the part too. The kid who said his father was some kind of important person in the drama department, and seemed to think that it was all decided, and he was going to be the one who would get the part.

William went on smiling after he'd started remembering the Bernard kid. It wasn't that he was gloating. At least not exactly. It was just . . . just what? Well, there was the fact that in his Baggetty past, he'd had lots of contests with kids who were bigger than he was. Pretty violent contests sometimes. And the other guy always won. Always. And now, in his fairly new existence as a Hardison, he'd apparently won one, against a kid who was not only bigger, but who had a father who was somebody important in the college drama department— instead of a good-for-nothing Baggett. So it was, under the circumstances, kind of hard not to smile—laugh out loud even. He stayed there on the bed for quite a while, then took a short impromptu nap, and when he woke up it was lunchtime, and he was still grinning.

The cafeteria was, he discovered, a pretty nice place to eat lunch. Breakfast too, probably, but that morning he'd been too busy dying of fright to notice. After he'd picked out a ham and cheese sandwich and some potato salad, he sat down at an empty table, but the place was pretty busy and before long some other people asked if they could join him. Two of them, a tall, stocky man and a woman with big eyes and lots of curly eyelashes. He nodded and they both smiled, and then the man said, "Let me guess. You must be our Puck. Right?"

William grinned and said, "That's right. How did you know?"

The woman rolled her big eyes before she said, "Oh, the word gets around pretty fast."

The man, who had a squarish head and a big, toothy grin, said, "Actually, casting results were posted in the greenroom an hour or so ago. So the word is out—the word about who got the roles that were still up for grabs until today. Which included who is to be our Puck. Very good." His grin had a sneaky edge to it as he added, "And even better, who isn't."

The woman shook her head and smiled as she said, "Now stop that." She turned to William and said, "My friend here was alluding to a young gentleman, who shall be nameless at the moment, who's been making a bit of a nuisance of himself lately by insisting he has the inside scoop on everything that's going on at the Mannsville Shakespeare Festival. Including who would be playing Puck."

William thought he could guess who she was talking about, but all he said was, "Yes, ma'am."

"So, your name is Hardison?" she asked.

"Yes, William Hardison."

She looked him over carefully and nodded. "Looks good to me, Mr. Hardison. Good typecasting, I'd say. And the word is, you can act, too."

Grinning, William said, "Good typecasting? You mean there's not enough here to be cast as a normal flesh-and-blood-type person?"

They both laughed out loud, and so did William. They went on chatting, and William learned that the woman's name was Virginia Blake and she would be playing Titania.

"Yes, Titania," she said. "Queen of the fairies, who falls madly in love with this guy here. Donkey head and all."

The guy then introduced himself to William as Tom Grant, and said he would be playing Bottom, the weaver. Of course William knew that Bottom was the character who got the donkey head, so he made a point of looking carefully at one side of the guy's head and then the other. And when the man asked, "Do you think I have the ears for it?" they all laughed again.

They were still laughing when suddenly Clarice Ogden, wearing lots of lipstick and a tight sweater, appeared out of nowhere. Putting down a trayful of dishes, she plopped herself down uncomfortably close to William.

"Hi, everybody," she said as she carefully arranged several plates of food in front of her in a neat semicircle. "I'm Clarice Ogden. Who are you?" She pointed at the man and then the woman. "Just you two, I mean." She leaned toward William and did a wide, slow smile. "I've known William for ages." There was something about the way she batted her eyes as she said it that made William's face begin to feel kind of warm.

After Virginia Blake/Titania and Tom Grant/Bottom introduced themselves, Virginia Blake asked Clarice if she was a member of the cast.

"Oh yes," Clarice said enthusiastically. "I'm going

to be Cobweb." She turned to William and asked, "You know about Cobweb?"

"One of Titania's fairies," he said, smiling and nodding in a way that must have been *too* knowing, because she shrugged.

"I know," she said. "You don't have to tell me. It's not a very big role. But it's not too bad. I even have some lines to say."

William's grin widened.

"Okay. Okay. Two words, but most of the fairies don't get to say anything. And there'll be really fabulous costumes, and Miss Scott says I can help with makeup, too. I'm good at makeup." She turned her attention back to Titania and Bottom then, and started explaining about how she was spending the summer with Miss Scott, one of the directors, who was a friend of her parents, and how her parents were both lawyers, and so on and so forth. And in the meantime William was trying to think of a reason he had to be somewhere else in a hurry.

He was still working on it when Bottom noticed that Clarice had two desserts—two slices of apple pie—and asked her if she had a sweet tooth.

"Well, I sort of do." She giggled. "But that piece"— she pointed to the bigger slice—"is for William." Doing another cutesy smile, she pushed it toward him. When he tried to say no thanks, she insisted. "I know you like sweet stuff, so when that lady behind the dessert counter wasn't looking, I snitched an extra piece for you."

Bottom and Titania were giving each other raised eyebrows and knowing smiles, and William was wishing there was some way he could tell them that what they were probably thinking wasn't anywhere near true, at least not where he was concerned. When Clarice went to get herself another Pepsi, Bottom grinned in a teasing way and said, "So, we seem to have another midsummer romance on our hands."

But Titania looked questioningly at William and asked, "Or perhaps"—she clasped her hands over her heart—"only another lovesick Helena?"

Bottom practically laughed his head off, but William didn't think it was funny. After telling Bottom and Titania that he had to go practice his lines, he quickly wrapped the extra piece of pie in his napkin and scooted for the door, and from there to his private room in Edwin Hall. His very private room.

Of course, saying he needed to practice his lines wasn't just an excuse. At least he made it the truth by going over Puck's act 2 speeches once again. And did a good job of it too, even with his mouth full of apple pie.

illiam's next journal entry began:

June 25, 1939

A lot of stuff has happened in the last few days. Some things I need to write out of my system and forget about. But also quite a lot of stuff that, years from now, I'll probably want to read over and over again. So here goes.

Monday was the first day of rehearsal, and I got to do Puck's long speeches at the beginning of act 2. Mr. Andre, the man with the beard who watched my audition, is the executive director, and everybody says he's pretty tough. He had me change some of the business I'd thought up. Some of the things I've been doing to break up Puck's long speeches. But he seemed to really like some other things I've been doing. I didn't notice, but Virginia Blake (the woman I met in *the cafeteria) told me that when I was doing one of the long speeches in act 2, she saw Mr. Andre nodding and laughing.*

*And after the rehearsal was over, he told me he's thinking of having Puck onstage in a few places where Shakespeare didn't mention it. Like I'll be sneaking around hiding behind bushes when the not-too-smart village craftsmen are making plans to put on the Thisbe play. I'll be watching what they're doing and falling all over myself laughing when they say dumb things. So I have a lot of new business to learn. Yesterday Mr. Andre had me do some handstands and backflips, and then he told me that since I was so acrobatic, he might have me enter once or twice by swinging onstage on a vine. Well, a rope actually, but they'll make it look like a vine. I'm to start practicing that tomorrow.*

A lot to practice and learn. William put down his pen as he thought about all the things he'd already learned in the first week of rehearsal. Days of shaking off attacks of stage fright, like always, before he went on, even though things always went pretty well once he got going. But there had also been a couple of backstage problems that he hadn't counted on. One of them was Clarice.

Clarice seemed to be backstage a lot, especially when

and where William wasn't expecting her to be. Like standing in the wings watching when he came offstage. On her way, she always told him, to get something for someone on the staff—like one of the set painters or stage crew. It seemed like she was always running errands that took her to wherever William happened to be.

There was the time, for instance, when he'd been called into the costume room, and the tall, long-fingered costume designer named Igor something-or-other was measuring him for his costume. William was standing on a stool in nothing but his underpants, while Igor wrapped tape measures around his chest and ran them up and down his legs, and just then the door opened and Clarice walked in, carrying a tray. William had his back turned when he heard her voice saying, "Hello there, Mr. Igor. Miss Walker just made a fresh pot of coffee, and I thought you might like some." And then, "Oh hi, William. I didn't know you were here. You want some coffee too?" Like it never occurred to her that a person standing on a stool with their clothes off might not be interested in coffee. At least not if it was being served by a person of the opposite sex.

Anywhere William went, it wasn't long before Clarice turned up. He also knew, even if Clarice didn't seem to, that the whole thing was getting to be a backstage joke. It was probably Bottom, the guy with the donkey head, who started it. He kept calling Clarice "Helena," and everybody seemed to get that the joke came from act 2, when the Helena character kept chasing after the guy named Demetrius, who kept trying to lose her. But Clarice didn't get it. She just went on reminding people, straight-faced, that her name was Clarice, not Helena.

William didn't think it was all that funny. For one thing, it wasn't that he hated Clarice, or anything like that. In fact, he still felt grateful about how she'd helped hide him and Jancy and the little kids in her basement when they were running away. So he really owed her a lot, even if she had told him and Jancy a few lies to keep them there when they really needed to get on with their escape. And of course he also owed her for the fancy new leather binder—which she'd sent him as a secret present, and then made it clear that she wanted him to know who it came from.

Actually, there were times, particularly when he was back in his room at night, when William kind of liked thinking that Clarice was crazy about him. It was just that when she showed up suddenly, batting her eyes and standing very close, it made him kind of nervous. He was going to work on it, though. And sometime soon, when he didn't have so many other things on his mind, he just might decide to tell her he liked her, too. It was an interesting thing to think about, but in the meantime he wished she'd stop, so Bottom and the rest of those jokers would stop teasing him.

And then there was Bernard. Bernard was another backstage problem that kept coming up. But in his case it definitely wasn't because he liked William too much. From William's point of view, Bernard was just looking for trouble. In fact, he as good as said so.

It was on the second full day of rehearsal and William, who was having a very busy day, had a break and went into the greenroom, the place where actors went to rest and relax. The greenroom at Mannsville was a really nice place. There were lots of chairs and couches, and over in one corner a little snack counter where there usually was hot water for coffee or tea, a soft-drinks refrigerator, and sometimes a few snacks. William checked out the snack counter—all gone—and then collapsed on one of the couches. Before he'd even had time to close his eyes, the door opened and Bernard walked in. William nodded and said hi, but Bernard didn't say anything. At least not right away. But later, when William's eyes were closed and he was half-asleep, a voice that came from very nearby said, "Hi, Hardison. Remember me?"

William opened his eyes, and there Bernard was, looking down at him. "Sure I do," William said. "You're Bernard." He sat up and, trying not to look or sound the least bit accusing, asked, "So, I guess you're in the cast too?" He didn't mean to rub it in or anything. It was a question that anybody might ask a person who was hanging out in a room that was supposed to be for cast members only.

But it was pretty obvious that Bernard didn't like the question. His teeth clenched, his big jaw got bigger, and his hands rolled into fists. Just at that moment a couple of other actors came in, which might have been the only reason that Bernard didn't do something more or less violent. But he did say something. What he said was, "Yeah, didn't you know? I'm your understudy."

Big relief. William swallowed hard and said, "Hey, that's great. I didn't know I had one. Nobody told me."

"Well, I am," Bernard said. "My dad and Mr. Andre have been talking about it. Actually, it looks like I'm going to be more than just an understudy. More like an alternate. You know about alternates?"

William thought he did. "It's someone who plays the role part of the time, instead of just when the lead actor is sick or something. Right?"

"Right. So maybe I'll sort of take over later in the summer. My dad and Mr. Andre are still discussing how much I'll be doing." Bernard seemed to be relaxing a little. His scowl had turned into a not-too-convincing grin. "In the meantime, I'll just be getting ready to take over suddenly if something should happen to you. You know, something unexpected. Got it?"

William got it. What he also seemed to be getting was that he'd better keep his eyes open when Bernard was around. Wide open.

William's journal entry that night covered all that

stuff. All about the new business he was supposed to learn, and a lot of other important problems that kept coming up. Problems, for instance, like Clarice and Bernard. It was fairly late at night when he wound up by writing:

> So that's the way things are going. I'm getting to know a bunch of the other actors and actresses. Of course, they're all pretty old, like in their twenties or thirties, or even older. All except Clarice—and Bernard, of course. But Miss Scott says that later on there will three or four other kids who will be playing Titania's fairies, and even one five-year-old kid who will be the changeling. The one that Titania and Oberon are fighting over. That should be kind of interesting, having a kid that little in such an important production.

Writing about a five-year-old made him think about Buddy. As he put the journal away and crawled into bed, he went on thinking about him, and of course Jancy and Trixie, too. He missed them. All of them. But it seemed like it was Buddy that he missed the most. He didn't know why, except maybe it was because he'd been the one who had been responsible for Buddy for so long. Especially in the old days when he had to get Buddy to the bathroom late at night, so the two of them wouldn't get beat on the next morning when Gertie found out he'd wet the bed. *Good old dead-to-the-world Buddy*, he was thinking as he pulled up the covers and settled down to sleep.

So it was sort of a coincidence that the very next evening, when he got back to Edwin Hall, the lady at the front desk handed him a letter that had arrived that day. It was from Jancy, and it was mostly about Buddy.

Of course, it wasn't the first letter that he'd received since he left Gold Beach. Just two days before Jancy's letter arrived, he'd gotten a short note from Aunt Fiona. One that they'd all signed. Even Buddy, in huge wobbly letters, and with the Ds backward so it actually said Bubby.

According to Aunt Fiona, they all missed him, but everyone was feeling well and enjoying the summer. But obviously that wasn't exactly the way Jancy saw it. Her letter went:

*Dear William,*

*I hope you are fine and having a good time. Everyone is okay here and we have done some fun things like going to the beach and the library. And Aunt Fiona says that next week, when* Rebecca of Sunnybrook Farm *comes to the Gold Beach Odeon, we can all go see it. As a reward* for being such good Hardisons. Buddy, too, even though <u>he doesn't deserve it.</u>

I'm worried about him, William. Things are happening just the way I was afraid they would as soon as you left. It's not just how he won't eat anything that's good for him, and doesn't come when Aunt Fiona calls him. Or even the way he is with the other neighborhood kids, like Freddie Burns and Bobby Johnson, who are both older than he is but not quite as big. Buddy keeps having fights with them. I'm not sure who starts the fights, but Buddy always wins them. I've tried to talk to Aunt Fiona about it, but she just doesn't take it very seriously. She just laughs and says things like "boys will be boys." Or that four is just a difficult age and that next year going to kindergarten will probably do a lot to civilize him.

William, what scares me is that he seems to be turning into a real Baggett. Of course, he can't help being big for his age, like most Baggetts. But what worries me is how much he acts like one.

Of course you probably won't agree with me, because he always behaves better when you are around. He used to mind me, too, or at least listen to me when I talked to him. Not anymore.

But maybe when you come home again things will be better. <u>If it's not too late by then</u>.

Please write to me.


Jancy


P.S. Buddy says for me to tell you that Pumpkin is just fine too.


William was glad and relieved to know that it was only Buddy who had been making Jancy so gloomy before he left home, and not something really scary—like for instance, something about the Baggetts. Not, he had to admit, that he'd spent much time worrying about them since he got to Mannsville. Not when he was awake, at least.

There had been some dreams, though. Nightmares, actually. Times when he'd awakened suddenly with his mind full of great dark Baggetty shadows. Threatening shapes that seemed to be chasing after him as he tried to run. Sometimes he'd be trying to hide under the bed in his room at Aunt Fiona's. But more often it would be right there at the Mannsville theater, where he would be trying to conceal himself backstage behind transparent stage sets and flimsy curtains, while huge Baggett-shaped creatures crept closer and closer. It was that one, the dream about Baggetts being right there, backstage in

Mannsville, that was the worst. As if it was warning him that he wasn't safe anywhere. That no matter where he went, Big Ed's belt was still waiting for him.

But none of his nightmares had been about Buddy. He sighed, feeling guilty. But then he shrugged, telling his conscience to get off his back. You couldn't blame him that much—what with all the things he'd had to cope with lately. Things like the audition, and then all the new stage business and blocking to memorize. He'd had all that stuff on his mind, not to mention Clarice, and Bernard.

He would write to Jancy right away. Just as soon as he reviewed what his promptbook said about the scenes they would be doing tomorrow. Mr. Andre had blocked out exactly where Puck was supposed to be and what he would be doing every second. Things like acting as if he couldn't believe his ears when Bottom and Quince were talking, and then laughing so hard he staggered around and then fell over backward. And where he would be, and how he would act when donkey-headed Bottom came onstage. There was a lot to memorize and practice, and by the time he'd finished he was really sleepy. He nodded firmly, telling himself he'd write the letter to Jancy tomorrow.

But tomorrow, as it turned out, was an even busier day. To begin with, it was the first rehearsal that included Titania's fairies—all of them. Clarice as Cobweb was the biggest one, but Peaseblossom and Moth were played by two really small kids. They were only about nine or ten years old. It must have been their first time onstage, and they were so nervous they kept stumbling over each other. Or getting so busy watching the other actors that they forgot to do anything.

But the biggest bottleneck was caused by the kid who was supposed to play the part of Titania's little changeling boy. His name was Jerry, and you might say his problem was that he wasn't nervous enough. He was having a great time, but what he definitely didn't get was that actors were supposed to listen to the director and do exactly what he tells them to do.

Mr. Andre probably would have dumped him right away, except he looked so great for the part, with a kind of movie-star kid face, and a whole lot of curly brown hair. But when he absolutely insisted on doing a Shirley Temple–style tap dance when he came onstage, it began to look like the director wasn't going to put up with him much longer. The kid's mother was right there in the wings, but he didn't listen to her, either. It was when Mr. Andre told everyone to take ten that William had a chance to talk to the kid.

What he did was to start a conversation that didn't sound like scolding, at least not at first, the way Jancy did sometimes with Trixie and Buddy.

Pulling the little show-off to one side, he said, "Hey, kid. You any good at pretending?"

"Yes, I am. I pretend better than anybody. Like when

I pretend I'm that tap dancer. I do that better than anybody."

"Yeah, I guess you do," William told him. "But the thing is, what we're doing here is this special pretend, see. Now the way *this* game goes is that that pretty lady"— he pointed to Titania—"is your mother, and that big guy is a really dangerous kidnapper. You know about kidnappers?"

The kid nodded, big-eyed.

"Yeah." William nodded back. He was pretty sure the kid would know about kidnappers. There'd been some pretty famous ones in the news lately. "Well, the way this game goes is that when the big guy says, '**I do but beg a little changeling boy,**' it means he's going to try to kidnap you and take you away to work for him. I mean like drag you off so you'll never see your mother again. And you *know* what he's up to. So that's when you're supposed to hang on to your mother's skirt and try to hide behind her and pretend you're scared to death. Looking scared to death when you really aren't is a hard thing to pretend. You think you could do it?"

Another big-eyed nod. And when the break was over, Jerry did just what he was supposed to do. Even looking wide-eyed and frightened. Problem solved. It turned out that Jerry really was good at pretending once he knew the story, and afterward he really liked all the praise he got for doing it so well.

When the rehearsal ended, and the kids were offstage, Mr. Andre called to William. "Hey, Hardison. How'd you like to double as an acting coach for all our preschool cast members?"

A lot of people laughed and clapped, and William laughed with them as he turned around, taking a few bows. However, as he turned past stage left he saw one face that wasn't exactly laughing, and farther out in the wings, another one that definitely wasn't. The first one was Clarice, and she was doing her fluttery-eyed stare, and the other face, the one that looked something like an angry bulldog, was Bernard Olson.

The rehearsal lasted until late that afternoon, and then Mr. Andre called a meeting to talk about the first run-through, which was scheduled for the day after tomorrow. He made a big point of repeating several times that they would be going through the whole play with no stopping, just as if it were opening night, no matter how many mistakes were made. "Absolutely no stopping, no matter how badly you mess up," Mr. Andre repeated. "Got it?"

William got it, along with a bad case of the willies that lasted right through dinner. Back in his room, he calmed himself down by going over his promptbook three or four times. It wasn't until late that night that he got around to writing the letter to Jancy.

Taking a page out of his journal, he began:

*Dear Jancy,*

*Thanks for writing. I'm sorry I didn't answer sooner but I've been awfully busy, and it looks like my schedule is going to get even harder.*

*I have been thinking about you, though. I was really worried when I was getting ready to leave for Mannsville, and you wouldn't tell me what was the matter. So now I know, and I don't really think you have all that much to be worried about. Not that I think it's okay for Buddy to act like a Baggett, because I don't. But don't you think it's a good sign that he wanted me to know that Pumpkin was okay? As you and I know, real Baggetts don't care what happens to guinea pigs.*

Oops! That was a mistake. Biting on the end of his pen, William read over what he had just written and wished he hadn't. Mentioning Jancy's first guinea pig's horrible fate was a pretty stupid thing to do in a letter that was supposed to cheer her up. But there it was, in unerasable ink. William stared at what he'd written, sighed, shrugged, and went on.

*Actually, I kind of agree with Aunt Fiona that being a pain in the neck is just something most boys have to go through at one time or another. And I also know that if anybody can straighten him out, it's you.*

Putting down his pen, William let his thoughts drift a little, but what they kept bringing up was all the stuff he ought to be practicing. So that was how it happened that the rest of the letter was mostly about blocking and stage business, and how Mr. Andre, the director, had given him—had given Puck, that is—so much extra stage business to do. And how day after tomorrow there was going to be the first run-through, which meant he couldn't go back and do it over if he messed up. Right at the end of the letter he did get back to the Buddy problem.

*About Buddy,* he finished up.

*Why don't you tell him one of your stories? Maybe you could make up one about the awful things that happen to people who don't eat their vegetables. Like maybe they shrivel up and turn into toothless monsters who can't eat anything but rotten tomatoes. And you can also tell him that William says for him to mind Aunt Fiona, and knock off picking on the neighbors' kids, or when I get home he'll have to listen to me practice Shakespeare for four hours every day. Okay?*

Then he addressed an envelope to Jancy Hardison. 971 Eleanor Street, Gold Beach, California, and went back to going over the stuff he would need to know tomorrow.

The way it turned out, William was only too right when he told Jancy that the next few days were going to be difficult. It was the very next morning that things started going wrong, when he somehow managed to lose his promptbook.

He'd written the promptbook in a little pocket-size tablet Miss Scott had given him. Each page started with his entry prompt, and then the beginning of each of the lines he had to say, along with charts that showed just where onstage he would be, and what he would be doing.

The charts were his own invention, and he felt good about the way they'd turned out. Below the words he had to say, he'd drawn little stick figures that reminded him what he was supposed to be doing at that moment. For instance, he'd drawn a little stick man lying on his back with his feet in the air when he was supposed to fall over backward laughing at the stupid things Bottom and Quince were saying. He'd put a lot of work into the promptbook, and even when there wasn't time to take it out and look at it, just knowing it was right there in his back pocket somehow made him feel a lot less nervous.

He knew the notebook had been in his pocket when he arrived at the greenroom that morning. He remembered taking it out on his way from the cafeteria to the theater, to check on his first entry in act 2. But a little later, when he was coming back from getting a doughnut at the snack counter, he reached in his pocket and discovered it wasn't there. He couldn't believe it. It wasn't the slippery kind of thing that would just fall out of a person's pocket. He checked his pocket again. No promptbook, and certainly no hole big enough for it to fall through.

By then nearly the whole cast was in the room, and it was pretty crowded, so he went around telling people he'd dropped an important little tablet that had all his cues in it, and asking them if they'd seen it. Nobody had, but when he told Titania (Virginia Blake), she started asking people to help look for it, and a few of them did, looking all over the floor and telling people to lift up their feet. But nobody found it. It was really weird, like it had somehow dissolved into thin air.

By then it was almost curtain time, and William had to get to the place in the left wing where he would make his first entrance—promptbook or no promptbook. He was on his way there when Clarice popped out from behind something, the way she was always doing, and said she was still looking for his promptbook. "I've been looking everywhere for it," she told him, smiling eagerly. "I'm sure I'll find it."

William was puzzled. "How'd you know about it?" he asked her. "You weren't in the greenroom when I lost it. At least I didn't see you."

She shook her head. "No, I wasn't. But Bernard was, and he told me you were asking people to look for it."

"Yeah, you're right. He was there. I saw him." William nodded thoughtfully. What he was remembering was that Bernard had been right behind him at the snack counter. It was something to think about.

Not that he had much time to think about it for the next few hours while the rehearsal was going on. But he did in bed that night, while he was trying to go to sleep. What kept going through his mind was how crowded it had been around the doughnut tray that morning, and whether someone who was sort of squeezed up behind him could have reached out and . . . Well, maybe not— but on the other hand . . .

The next morning as he walked from Edwin Hall to the cafeteria, he was still trying to decide whether to say anything to Bernard. Not that he'd have to decide right away since Bernard never ate at the cafeteria, because he lived with his parents right there on campus. There would be time later to decide whether to accuse him of taking the tablet.

What he should do right at that moment, he told

himself, was just forget about it, at least for the time being. So that was what he did.

Once the curtain went up that afternoon on the important first run-through, William's mind definitely wasn't on what Bernard might or might not have done. Or even on what was missing from his rear pocket. As the play began he didn't have any trouble remembering where he was supposed to be and what he had to do and say. In act 1 when the villagers were trying to organize their crazy play, it was easy for William to remember the extra business that Mr. Andre had given him to do.

William thought that part came off pretty well, but then came the beginning of act 2, where Mr. Andre had come up with some really special stuff. The way it was staged, the act 2 curtain went up on a woodsy scene that looked like a clearing in a deep forest. And then Puck would swing in on a rope and circle around like a trapeze artist, before he dropped down midstage. Eventually the rope was going to be decorated with lots of fake leaves to make it look like a forest vine, but so far it was just an especially heavy cord. After William arrived onstage, he was to prance around playing to the audience, mugging and grinning, and doing backflips and handstands, until the First Fairy entered, stage left. Then he was to strut over to her, make a fancy bow, and start his big act 2 speech.

He had rehearsed the rope-swinging entry dozens of

times without any problem, and he was feeling Puckishly confident and cocky as he grabbed the rope and launched himself off from halfway up a tall backstage ladder. But this time something was different. Terribly different.

For some reason he couldn't seem to hold his grip. His hands slipped, and even though he hung on for dear life, he kept on sliding down the rope until, instead of soaring in a wide circle, he landed on the stage with a thud. Not hard enough to do much damage, but hard enough to hurt some, and ruin the whole effect. And because it was a run-through, he couldn't go back and do it over to get it right.

He filled in the best he could by going ahead with the acrobatics, but it wasn't easy, because he'd landed hard enough to twist his left ankle a little, and it was hurting. But at least he didn't forget his lines. When the First Fairy came in, he said the stuff about Titania's changeling boy and then about being a **"merry wanderer of the night."** But he was really glad to get to **"Here comes Oberon"** and limp offstage.

Once he was in the wings, Miss Scott and several other people rushed up to ask him if he was all right. And Tom Grant insisted on taking off his shoe and examining his ankle. William kept saying he was fine, and by then he really was, at least physically. But he was really embarrassed about messing up something he thought was going to be exciting and a lot of fun.

The rest of the performance went all right and William, even without his promptbook, managed to get through it without making any more mistakes. But he still felt bad about goofing up his big entry. The worst part, though, was when the final curtain came down, and Mr. Andre came looking for him and insisted on looking at his ankle.

"What do you think, Hardison?" he asked. "Maybe we ought to forget your airborne entry. We don't want you to risk life and limb just to give our audiences a brief thrill. Now, do we?"

"No, sir. I mean, yes, sir," William stammered. "I mean, I really want to do it. I've done it lots of times without any trouble at all. I don't know what went wrong, but I don't think it will happen again. It just seemed like the rope was extra slippery or something. I don't think it will be so slippery once it has the leaves and stuff on it."

"Well," Mr. Andre finally said, "we'll have to give it some more thought, and maybe have Fred look into it tomorrow morning. There must have been some reason for the difference."

"That's a good idea," William agreed. Fred Bloom was the head man in the stage crew who took care of all the sets and props. "Maybe he can find out why the rope was so slippery."

Mr. Andre got up, saying, "I'm late for a staff meeting. Are you all right to walk back to your dorm?"

William jumped up and bounced on both feet. "Sure," he said. "See! My ankle's fine. I'm just fine, sir."

And he was. Not much ankle pain, but his messed-up entry was still very much on his mind. And the more he thought about it, the more certain he became that he was going to need to look into it, with Mr. Bloom's help or not. And to do that right away, it was going to be necessary for him to hang around for a while after everyone else cleared out. Not in the greenroom, because he didn't want people asking about his ankle. Instead he looked around for a good hiding place, somewhere nearby, but out of sight.

He checked out several possibilities, where set builders and janitors were still at work. Then as he passed the costume room, he opened the door and peeked in. Nobody there. Nothing but rows and rows of costumes hanging on metal racks. So he scooted in, past long rows of Shakespearean-looking stuff—surcoats and jerkins, doublets and bodices, and even a fairly convincing suit of armor. He kept on going until he found what he was looking for. A good hiding place, behind several long robes that hung clear down to the floor. Well hidden among folds of velvet, he crouched down and waited. And went on waiting until the sounds from the stage slowly faded and then died away completely. It wasn't until the silence had lasted for several minutes that he stood up and, pushing aside a fur-trimmed robe, peered out. Nobody there. Good.

While putting the robe back in place, he couldn't

help but notice how grand it looked. And how good it felt when he wrapped its long, velvety length around his shoulders, with the fur-trimmed collar brushing against his neck. Standing tall, he tried a few slow paces and then, still moving with regal dignity, made his way down the aisle and out to the fitting room, with its long mirrors. Turning from side to side, he admired the effect of wearing a royal robe. It was a lot different from the tights and tunics that he'd worn as Ariel, and the outfit that Igor was putting together for Puck was going to be just as skimpy.

William decided he liked the difference. He practiced a few royal poses, shoulders back and high, head up. Not bad, he thought, particularly with the padded velvet thickening his chest and shoulders. Someday he might do one of Shakespeare's kings—like one of the Henrys. But then, reminding himself of why he was there, he stopped fooling around and got down to business. Back in the costume room, he hung up the robe and headed for the deserted stage.

It was almost dark backstage now, and very quiet. Walking quickly, William made his way through a forest of fake trees and behind some almost transparent leafy scrims. He was halfway across the stage when all of a sudden something made him stop and crouch down behind a small cardboard bush. Peering out, he frantically looked for . . . for what?

Nothing and nobody there. It was, he decided, just the memory of that dream. That stupid nightmare that kept coming back, about a bunch of Baggetts chasing him around backstage. "Forget it," he told himself. "It was just that silly dream. You're in Mannsville now, not Crownfield. See,"—he looked around—"no Baggetts here." Shaking his head hard, he stepped out from behind the bush and started taking firm, determined steps until he came to the ladder that led up to his takeoff spot. He stopped once more to look and listen.

Complete silence. Still favoring his left ankle a little, he slowly and carefully began to climb the ladder.

Midway up the tall ladder there was just room enough for a person to turn around, reach up overhead, and unhook the rope. He'd done it so many times before, it had become almost automatic. And now, reaching out into near darkness, it was reassuring to find that the rope had been replaced on its hook. Which must mean that one of the stagehands had climbed up and replaced it, as they always did at the end of act 2. There it was, right where it was supposed to be, and always had been when Puck reached up to grab it and take off on his soaring entry.

Lifting the rope off the hook, William ran his hands up and down its rough, scratchy surface. It felt familiar—the same as always—or maybe, not quite? There was—what? A slightly increased slippage, as his hand moved up and down. Almost as if . . . He was still wondering just what the difference was when he noticed something else. A smell.

William had always had a sensitive nose. A nose that

had reacted strongly to such things as the stifling, musty odor of his attic hideout at the Baggetts, and later to the clean, fresh smell of Aunt Fiona's house. And now his nose was telling him that there was a smell up there, halfway up the backstage ladder, that seemed to be coming from the rope itself.

Lifting it to his nose, he breathed deeply—sniffed and sniffed again. And then he knew. It was a familiar smell, one that usually made his mouth water a little. He swallowed hard. What the rope smelled like was definitely—bacon. William sniffed again, and nodded. No doubt about it, the rope smelled like bacon.

Standing on tiptoes, he smelled again farther up, beyond where his hands usually reached. No. Only a bit of dusty dryness. No bacon there. And no slippery smoothness, either. But down where he usually held the rope, he could still feel a slight, slippery difference.

Grabbing the rope with both hands, as he always did before he pushed off, William leaned back on his heels, testing his grip. There was a bit of a slip, but not much. Not nearly as much as he remembered feeling when he'd confidently swung off into space that afternoon— and found himself sliding on down the rope until he landed, too soon and much too hard. Which could mean that in the meantime someone had wiped it clean, at least as much as was possible.

It was then that William began to put it all together.

Since that afternoon, when he'd made his embarrassing crash landing, somebody must have come backstage, climbed up the ladder, and carefully wiped off as much of the . . . the what?

Yeah. He had it. Bacon grease. Somebody had wiped off most of the bacon grease that it had been smeared with. Probably the same person who sometime earlier had put a thick layer of grease just where William's hands would grab hold. And it didn't take much longer to figure out who that someone must have been.

After all, who would be only too happy if William Hardison broke an arm or an ankle, and wasn't able to play the role of Puck on opening night? And—another important point—what person actually lived, not in a kitchenless dormitory, but in his parents' home? In a home where quite possibly this person's mother saved bacon grease, like Aunt Fiona did, to use for frying potatoes and things like that? And what if this same person arrived backstage early and climbed up to grease the strip of rope right where William's hands went when he started his swing? And who then could have hung around long enough to find an opportunity to wipe off as much of the remaining grease as possible, to keep anyone from finding out what he had done?

As he climbed down and quickly and quietly made his way to the stage door, William was congratulating himself on good detective work. He was clear out the door and heading across the parking lot before it came to him that what his detective work didn't and couldn't tell him was what to do next. What would happen, for instance, if he went to Miss Scott, or even Mr. Andre, and told them what had caused his embarrassing foul-up, and who he thought was responsible?

Would they believe him? The bacon grease was pretty much gone now, and by tomorrow the smell would probably be too. So wouldn't Mr. Andre, and probably Miss Scott, too, suspect that William's wild story was just something he'd made up? A kind of alibi so he could say that it hadn't been his fault and blame everything on somebody else. On someone who, as everyone knew, wasn't exactly a friend of his. And quite likely a person that Mr. Andre would think twice about accusing, since his father was an important person at Mannsville College. Maybe even one of the big shots who decided whether the Shakespeare festival could be held on the college campus every summer . . .

By the time William reached the dormitory, he was beginning to think he'd better keep his mouth shut about his suspicions. Just say nothing at all. And do nothing, except try to keep his eye on Bernard as much as possible.

That night at the cafeteria William sat at the same table as Quince and Bottom, and a couple of other members of the cast. Good friends, especially Bottom, who was trying to be comforting about the accident. But most of all, he seemed to be concerned that Mr. Andre might not let William go on making his flying entrance. He was grinning as he said, "If I were our fairly famous director, I'd insist that you continue doing your Tarzan-type entry, broken ankles or not."

"No kidding, William," he went on, "we've all seen you do it dozens of times without any problem. And I'm sure it's going to be one of those wild applause moments that the Mannsville festival is so famous for. You'll see. Just wait until all the important critics and reviewers have their say. I can see it all now."

Putting a pompous, self-important look on his funny face, Tom Grant/Bottom held out an imaginary newspaper and pretended to read, "As always this year's Mannsville's Shakespeare was more or less entertaining, but what made this summer's effort call for a real standing ovation was the kid who played Puck, who is obviously going to be the next Johnny Weissmuller."

William got the point. Way back when he used to go to the movies in Crownfield, he'd seen a lot of Tarzan movies, with an actor named Johnny Weissmuller swinging on the jungle vines, along with Cheetah, his pet chimpanzee.

So now William grinned back and asked, "Or maybe the next Cheetah?" They all cracked up laughing, saying things like, "Good one, Hardison," and "You tell him, Puckster."

By the time William went back to the dorm that night,

he was feeling pretty good about himself. But later, in bed and trying to sleep, he began thinking again about Bernard and what he *maybe*, or *probably*, or *pretty much for sure*, had done. Thinking about what kind of a person would set a trap that might hurt somebody, even hurt them really bad, just because they'd been given a part he wanted and thought was his.

It was all pretty frustrating. Insomnia had never bothered William. Lying in bed for hours without being able to go to sleep wasn't something he'd done much of, not even when he was still a Baggett, freezing or roasting in a crummy attic. But now, thinking about Bernard's dirty trick, and how there was no way he, William, was going to be able to do anything about it, was enough to make his eyes refuse to stay closed for more than a minute or two at a time.

Because he was tired of staring at the ceiling, he got out of bed pretty early the next morning and made his way to the cafeteria, feeling groggy and bleary-eyed. And since there was no one there to talk to at that hour, it didn't him take long to eat. Which meant he got to the theater quite a bit earlier than usual, and when he walked into the greenroom he discovered that there were only a few people there. And one of them was Clarice.

Rats. In love with him or not, Clarice Ogden was not someone he was in any mood to cope with right at that moment. Curled up in one of the big easy chairs, she looked up when he came in, quickly got to her feet, and hurried toward him. William glanced around, hoping to locate someone else he just had to talk to immediately. No such luck.

Clarice kept coming, and when she was practically standing on his toes she began to whisper. "Guess what. I found out something very important. Something you need to know."

"Oh yeah?" William said. "Like what?"

She rolled her eyes, looking around the room suspiciously, as if she were afraid someone might be listening. "It's about your notebook."

What immediately came to mind was that Clarice was referring to the leather-bound binder she'd sent him last fall. "Oh, that," he said. "You don't have to tell me. I guessed. There wasn't any return address on the package, but I guessed you must have sent it."

For a moment she stared at him blank-eyed, before she started to shake her head. "No, no. I didn't mean that notebook. I meant the little one you carried around in your pocket. The one you were looking for yesterday."

"Oh, you mean my *prompt*book? Okay, I got it now. You mean you know what happened to it?"

"Yes, I do." She nodded firmly. "It was Bernard. I think he tore it up."

"He tore it up?" William gasped. "What makes you think so?"

Clarice was still nodding. "I'm pretty sure. You know that blue and gold Mannsville College sports jacket he wears sometimes? The one that he usually hangs down at the end of the coatroom? Well, when I was leaving last night I went in there to get my sweater, and I noticed two little scraps of paper down at the end of the room—right below Bernard's jacket. And here they are."

Reaching in her pocket, Clarice fished around and brought out two small pieces of paper. "See. Look at this."

William looked. The scraps weren't very big, but there was enough for him to be able to see that the handwriting was his. And the little sketch of a stick figure making a bow was a reminder of what he had to do in act 5 at the end of the play.

"Yeah," he said between clenched teeth. "That's my promptbook. Part of it, anyway."

He wasn't used to feeling angry. At least not the kind of anger that boiled up inside you and made you want to yell and punch something, or maybe even somebody. Somebody like that mean, sneaky, pickpocket Bernard Olson. But he felt that way now, and that must have been what caused him to say something that, only a second later, he knew was a huge mistake.

What he said was, "So that's what he did right before he tried to kill me."

ried to kill you?" Clarice was staring at him
goggle-eyed. "What . . . ? When . . . ? What
are you talking about?"

"Shh." William looked around to see if anyone else
had heard. No one seemed to be listening. "I shouldn't
have said that," he went on. "I don't know for sure if he
did it. I mean, not really."

"Did it? Did what?"

"Well, it's just that I think that yesterday someone
put bacon grease on my rope. Someone climbed up and
greased it right where I grab it when I swing off. And
that's why I slid down like that and made a mess of my
entrance. And almost broke my ankle."

Clarice was wide-eyed, her hands over her mouth.
After she'd gasped a few more times, she said, "You told
them, didn't you? I mean, Mr. Andre and all of them. You
did, didn't you?"

"Well, no. I haven't yet. I was going to, but then I
thought, I don't have any proof. By the time I went up to

investigate, someone had already been there and wiped it pretty clean. But I could still smell it. The bacon, I mean. But by now the smell is probably pretty much gone too. I decided that if I started telling people, they'd just think I was trying to blame someone else for my own goof-up."

Clarice was still staring at him over her clasped hands. "But you have to," she said. "You have to tell them, or he'll just keep on trying to kill you."

"No!" William shook his head firmly. "I told you, I decided it wouldn't do any good. I don't have any proof, and he'd just deny everything. And it would only be my word against his."

"Then I'll tell them."

"No. No. No." Leaning closer, he whispered, "They wouldn't believe you, either." He was thinking about how everyone would react if Clarice started blaming Bernard for William's accident. Bottom, Tom Grant that is, was still calling Clarice "Helena" because he thought she was crazy about William—like Helena was about Demetrius in the play. So everyone would just think she was trying to prove the accident wasn't his fault because she was in love with him. They wouldn't believe her any more than they'd believe William himself. But he wasn't going to bring that up at the moment. So all he could do was shake his head and keep repeating, "They wouldn't believe you. So don't do it. Please don't. Please!"

Clarice's eyes had narrowed to angry slits as she said,

"Okay. I won't tell Mr. Andre, or Miss Scott, but I *am* going to tell someone." She put her hands on her hips. "You know who? Well, I'm going to tell Mr. Bernard Olson himself. I'll tell him that we know what he's been doing, and he'd better stop it. Or else!" And before William could stop her, she had whirled around and stomped out the door.

William looked around the greenroom. There still wasn't a large crowd, and no one seemed to be watching him. No one, that is, except Tom Grant, who was grinning at William and raising his bushy eyebrows in a kind of teasing way, probably getting ready to say some 𝕾𝖍𝖆𝖐𝖊𝖘𝖕𝖊𝖆𝖗𝖊 quote about a lovers' quarrel.

William turned his back on Tom and strolled over to the call-board, in what was supposed to be a relaxed, unconcerned way. But if Tom, or anybody else who might be watching at that moment, thought William looked the least bit relaxed, it was just one more proof that he, William 𝕾. Hardison, was a natural-born actor. Standing in front of the call-board and pretending to calmly read the notices, what he was really thinking was, *That does it. Now everything is going to fall apart. Clarice is going to find Bernard and tell him that she—that she and I—think that he stole my promptbook and tore it up, and tried to kill me by putting grease on my entry rope. And then he, Bernard, will . . . he will . . . do what?*

For a minute or two that was as far as his thinking

went. What *would* Bernard do after Clarice told him? Would he go to Mr. Andre and tell him that Clarice and William were trying to blame William's accident on him just because they didn't like him?

It took only a minute for William to decide that no, probably Bernard wouldn't do that. Because when Mr. Andre wanted to know exactly what they were saying about him, Bernard would have to tell him, wouldn't he? And then Mr. Andre would probably feel it was something he had to look into a little more carefully. Like maybe hiring a professional detective who had ways to tell if bacon grease had been on a rope, even after it had been carefully wiped away. No, William decided, if he had any sense at all, Bernard probably wouldn't tell anyone just what he was being accused of. So what else could he do?

While he was still standing there, pretending to read things on the call-board and thinking about what Bernard might do, William finally came to the conclusion that Bernard just might not do anything at all. He might feel that it would be too risky for him to tell anybody about what Clarice had accused him of. So maybe, just maybe, it wasn't such a dangerous situation after all, because another possibility was that when Bernard found out that William and Clarice were onto him, he might not have the nerve to try anything else.

It wasn't until he'd gotten that far in his thinking

that William actually did start to read the notices on the bulletin board, and found out that there was to be a cast meeting in about twenty minutes. A very important meeting in which there would be a discussion about the first dress rehearsal, which was scheduled for the day after tomorrow, as well as a reminder that opening night was only a few days after that. A reminder important and exciting enough to make William forget all about Bernard, at least for the next few minutes.

So William went to the cast meeting and learned that all the costumes were finished and that appointments had been made for final fittings, and that the stage crew were about to put together the last of the sets. And then, just as he was leaving, Mr. Andre called to William. "Hey, Hardison," he said. "I want you to come with me right now and let me watch you do your flying entry one more time. And if there doesn't seem to be any problem, some prop people will be put to work immediately turning your rope into a vine, and we'll go ahead with it as planned."

William said, "Okay," as if he really meant it, and this time he definitely wasn't acting.

Out on the stage Mr. Andre had some crew guys bring out a big thick pad and spread it out where William had crash-landed the day before. "Just in case," he said. And then he stood there watching with his fierce eyebrows bunched together and his hands on his hips, while William climbed up to his takeoff spot and quickly tested for the smell or feel of bacon grease. Not a bit of either one.

Then, feeling not at all nervous, he grabbed the rope, called, "Okay. Here I come," and swung out and away. Swung out, twisting to one side and then the other to build up momentum, and then back again to land lightly center stage, and start strutting and cartwheeling and doing flips as he always did while he waited for the First Fairy to appear.

Mr. Andre's little white beard bobbed up and down as he nodded, clapped, and shouted, "Bravo! Well done." Then he motioned to some stage crew guys who had been watching from the wings, and called, "Get that rope over to the prop people and tell them we'll be expecting a convincingly leafy vine by tomorrow afternoon."

And also by tomorrow afternoon William had been assigned not only his own dressing room but also a dresser. A man named Mr. Leroy Turner, who taught things like costumes and makeup in the drama department at Mannsville College and who was, according to greenroom gossip, the best dresser you could hope for.

"Shows how important the powers that be think you are in this production," Tom Grant told William. "So appreciate him."

William said he would, but until that evening he

didn't know how much. After Mr. Turner finished with him, and William finally got to check himself out in a full-length mirror, he was astonished by what he saw. Dressed in a tight-fitting tunic that seemed to be made out of big green leaves, with his eyes lengthened and darkened, his eyebrows painted into sweeping arches, and with his elf ears reaching so far up past the top of his head they looked like antennas, he hardly recognized himself. He looked, not like Willy Baggett for sure, and not even like a sometimes shaky and uncertain William Hardison, but quite a bit like an unreal fairy-tale creature known, for some reason, as Robin Goodfellow, or sometimes just as Puck.

"How do you like it?" Mr. Turner asked.

"It's great. I mean, I hardly recognize myself. You did a great job," William said.

Leroy Turner grinned. "You're right. I did. But I had some good raw material to work with. You have great cheekbones, kid, and a smile that's pure electricity."

William was still wondering about the electric smile thing as he was leaving the dressing room and heading for stage left. He was, that is, until someone poked him in the back, and he turned around to see an unfamiliar creature with a painted face, wearing a kind of tutu and a pair of gauzy wings that floated out behind her back. It took him a couple of seconds to realize he was looking at Clarice Ogden.

"William?" she asked as if she weren't quite sure.

"Hi, Cobweb," he said, grinning.

She nodded, but she didn't smile back. Instead her eyes narrowed into mascara-fringed slits as she said, "I told him. I really talked to Bernard. And I told him that we know all about what he did."

For the first few seconds after Clarice told him what she had done, William felt as if he'd been thumped in the chest. Thumped so hard the breath was pretty much knocked out of him, so the dress parade and the important dress rehearsal didn't get off to a very relaxed start. At least not as far as William was concerned.

So Bernard knew. Knew that William and Clarice had found out that he was the one who, not only stole and tore up an important little notebook, but also did something that might have caused a broken arm or leg, or even a neck. But what nobody knew was what he would decide to do next.

On the one hand, you might think that knowing he'd been found out might make Bernard afraid to try any other tricks. But on the other hand, a person who'd had as much experience with *natural-born bullies* as William knew one when he saw one, even if his father was Dean of Performing Arts at Mannsville College. And he also knew that such a person, given the chance to do serious damage, usually just went ahead and did it—no matter what the consequences might be.

Right at that moment, however, before there was time for William to do or say anything, the backstage lights flashed three times—the signal that the dress parade was about to begin.

Shoving not only Bernard the rope greaser, but also Clarice the blabbermouth, out of his mind, William hurried to get in place for the dress parade. All the actors circled around the stage, checking one another out and having fun reacting to everybody's transformation into Shakespearean characters. Especially to Bottom, who had chosen to wear his donkey head as he paraded, and almost as much to Puck, with his arched eyebrows and antenna ears. But then there were three more flashes, and the stage cleared for the beginning of the dress rehearsal.

So the curtain went up and dress rehearsal began— and went well for everybody. Especially William S. Hardison. William knew it before anyone told him so, and a lot of people did tell him. He knew it by the way that he had not only looked like, but also felt like, Puck whenever he was onstage. Felt like a mischievous, limber-legged show-off, as he pranced around reciting all the lines Shakespeare had given Puck to say, as well as adding all the extra stage business that Mr. Andre had thought up for him to do. Not to mention making his fancy flying entrance in act 2, when he flipped and twirled like a trapeze artist, with not a bit of slippage. And afterward everyone, not only Miss Scott and all the cast but also a lot of backstage people—dressers, and set crews, and even one of the campus police officers, a huge man named Sergeant Blanding—came to his dressing room to tell him how well he'd done. It was all pretty exciting.

When he finally got back to his room that night, there was another letter from Jancy. William sighed, shook his head, and tried to get his mind out of its excited whirlwind and down to what his sister had to say. This time the letter started out with some good news, but just like before it ended with a bunch of stuff about Buddy and the problems he'd been causing.

Dear William, it began:

I guess you must be really busy now that the play is about to start. Opening night is real soon, isn't it? I think it must be a very exciting time for you. Please write and tell me all about it. I have some swell news. Aunt Fiona says that if she can afford to get the car's brakes fixed, we, all four of us, will drive down to Mannsville to see you being Puck. She says it would be swell if we could stay for closing night so you could ride back home with us. Would you like that?

Aunt Fiona is going to write to Miss Scott and ask her if she could find us a not-too-expensive place to stay for a couple of nights. Do you think she could?

Now the not-so-good news. Buddy still is being a big problem. All the time!!! Last Thursday he let Tiger, you know, the Johnsons' cocker spaniel, into the kitchen and put him under the table. And when Aunt Fiona put some string beans on Buddy's plate, he sneaked them down to Tiger, one at a time when she wasn't looking. I saw what he was doing, but I didn't tell on him, but Trixie did. Aunt Fiona scolded him a little, but when she said she was going to punish him by not letting him have dessert he howled, and she went ahead and let him have some.

And then yesterday he gave Aunt Fiona ~~some chrisansomoms~~ some crysanthamums (can't spell them). Anyway, those big yellow flowers, and told her he bought them for her at the florist's with some money he earned by pulling weeds in Mrs. Howard's garden. But Mrs. Howard told me that Buddy picked the chris (whatevers) in her garden all right, without asking permission, and if he pulled some weeds she was glad, but nobody *told him to, or paid him for doing it. So you see how it is, and why I'm still very worried about him.*

*Jancy*

The letter made William feel guilty. Guilty because he found it so difficult to get his mind away from his great dress rehearsal and down to writing an answer. And also because when he read over what Buddy had done, he found it hard to take it as seriously as Jancy obviously thought he should. In fact, he couldn't help grinning a little when he pictured Buddy trying to look innocent as he slipped string beans, one by one, under the table and into Tiger.

But he didn't say so. Actually, he didn't say much. He just wrote a very short note, saying he thought it was swell that they were all going to be able to come for closing night, and that he could see why she was worried about Buddy. That was about all he had to say, except he added in a P.S. that he didn't think he could spell those big yellow flowers either. Of course there was that big dictionary on his desk, but he just wasn't in the mood to worry about how to spell an ordinary garden flower.

The next day there were only special rehearsals of some scenes that Mr. Andre thought needed extra work, and none of them were William's, so he more or less had the day off. But he went to the greenroom anyway, because there wasn't anything else to do. And because it was fun talking to people who happened to come in. Like Miss Scott, for instance.

William was sitting at one of the tables when she came in, and he didn't see her until she came up behind him and put her hands on his shoulders. When he turned around she gave him a big smile and said, "I'm so pleased, William. You were marvelous. Even better than I expected."

William didn't think he was the blushing type, but his face did get kind of hot, and for a minute he couldn't think of anything to say. Then he grinned and said, "Good typecasting, I guess. Guess I'm just the not-exactly-human type. You know, Ariel first and now Puck."

She patted his shoulder again and said, "Don't you believe it. Wait a few years and we'll be casting you as Romeo, or maybe Henry the Fifth." She started to go away and then turned back to say, "Besides, don't put yourself down for being out of the ordinary. I think this world could use a few more original, outside-the-mold types."

She went away then, and William went back to saying thanks to people who came in and said things like, "Nice going, kid," and "You're going to kill 'em, Puckster."

When the greenroom door opened again and Bernard came in, William caught his breath. Before he could look away, Bernard gave him what almost looked like a smile, and said, "Congratulations, William. Good job."

He couldn't believe it! Congratulations, and good job? From Bernard? William was so surprised his mouth must have hung open for a few seconds before anything came out. But he finally managed, "Thanks. Thanks a lot."

Bernard didn't stay long, but he left William wondering. Wondering why a guy who had almost always been rude would suddenly change to being almost friendly to someone he knew had accused him of stealing and trying to cause a serious accident.

Sitting there in the greenroom, in between chatting with people who wanted to tell him how well he'd done last night, William went on wondering exactly what Clarice had told Bernard. Did she make him think she and William were waiting to see what he might do next before they told on him? Or else did she threaten him with something that scared him so much he decided to reform? Because exactly what she'd said, and how she said it, might explain why Bernard suddenly seemed to be a normal person, or at least someone who could act like one.

The more he thought about it the more anxious William became to talk to Clarice and find out exactly what she'd said to Bernard. But as it happened, Clarice's Cobweb scene, the one with all of Titania's fairies, was one that needed some extra rehearsals that morning. So the only way William was able to see her was from the wings as she flitted around the stage with the other fairies. He was still waiting for a chance to talk to her when one of the stagehands rushed up and said that Mr. Andre was looking for him.

William couldn't imagine why, since he'd been told that he didn't need to report that day. But he soon found out. In the greenroom, the first thing he saw—and heard—was little old Jerry, the changeling, who was sitting on the floor in the middle of the room, screaming his head off. Around him in a circle were Mr. Andre, Miss Scott, Jerry's mother, and two or three other frantic-looking people. Jerry, who had been given the role of Titania's changeling because he looked so angelic, had spells of acting pretty devilish, and more than once before William had been the only one who could talk him out of whatever he was doing. Mr. Andre said it was another of William's exceptional talents. So now they were counting on him to do it again.

He'd been watching for more than a minute before anyone noticed that he was there, but when Mr. Andre did, he motioned for William to come over. The director's lips were tight and thin, and his bushy eyebrows were practically standing on end as he pulled William aside and whispered, "That little monster is having another tantrum. I'd dump him for sure, but it seems his understudy has the mumps. Can you talk to him? Think you could get to him to listen to reason?"

William said, "Gee, Mr. Andre. I don't know if I can. But I'll try."

The kid seemed pretty wound up. But then William remembered something he'd seen Jancy do when Buddy was having a fit about something. So he went over and sat down right in front of Jerry, leaned forward, crossed his eyes, pushed up the end of his nose, and let his tongue loll sideways out of his mouth. Jancy called it making a gargoyle face, and sometimes it worked for Buddy. Sure enough, after a couple of minutes Jerry stopped screaming, gulped, and demanded, "Why are you doing that?"

And William grinned and said, "Doing what? I wasn't doing anything."

When Jerry started to scream again, William made another horrible face, and before long Jerry stopped to watch. After this happened once or twice more, Jerry wiped the tears off his face, got to his feet, and making a wide circle around William, went over to Miss Scott. When she put out her hand, he took it and let her lead him out the door. And a few minutes later, when it was his turn to be onstage, he wiped his face again and did what he was supposed to.

Watching from the wings, Mr. Andre turned to William and said, "Well, young man, you do have a lot of tricks up your sleeve. Where did you learn that one?"

When William said he'd learned it from his sister, Mr. Andre smiled and nodded. "I see. You obviously come from an unusually talented family."

William only grinned and said, "Yeah, I guess you could say that," and went back to looking for Clarice.

She wasn't in the greenroom or anywhere backstage. It wasn't until he'd almost given up and was on his way to the cafeteria that he saw her up ahead of him. He managed to catch up just as she was going through the door.

"Hey, Clarice," he called, and she stopped, turned back, and waited. She had a different look. Like she had on some leftover stage makeup, maybe? But there was more to it than that. Something about the tight-lipped, narrow-eyed way she was looking at him?

"What do you want?" Her tone of voice had changed too. He had expected—what? He wasn't sure.

"I have to talk to you." He looked around to be sure no one was going to overhear. The other fairies she'd been walking with had gone on into the cafeteria. "I want to know what you told Bernard, and what he said. You know—the promptbook thing, and the bacon grease? Did he admit it?"

Clarice's strangely blank stare continued as she said, "Well, sort of, I guess. We haven't finished discussing it. What do you want to know?"

"Well, what he said, and how he acted when you told him. Because I can't figure him out. He's, I don't know—not the same. He's acting different."

Clarice nodded. "I know. He is different. We're talking about it." Then she whirled around and went on into the cafeteria. And left William just standing there thinking and wondering.

Obviously he'd done something that hurt Clarice's feelings a lot. He couldn't imagine what it could have been, but then if Jancy was right about Clarice being in love with him, that might explain it. From what he'd heard and read about people who were in love, it seemed that they were often kind of touchy about how the person they loved ought to be treating them.

*That's probably it,* he told himself. *I probably did something stupid without meaning to, and if she would just tell me what it was I would say I was sorry and try not to do it again.* He was still trying to figure out what it might have been as he went on down the path to the cafeteria, went in, and sat down where he didn't have to look toward Clarice and she didn't have to look at him.

The next night William got out his secret journal and did some writing. It had been quite a while since his last entry. When he'd brought his journal with him to Mannsville, he thought he'd be writing in it every night, but it hadn't turned out that way. He wasn't exactly sure why. Of course, part of it was that he'd had too much else to do. But there was more to it than that.

One of the reasons he used to need to write so often when he was still a Baggett was that there had been so much that he needed to put down on paper, in order to get it off his back. It sometimes helped quite a bit. After putting a bunch of the worst stuff down in pen and ink, it was kind of like he'd written it out of his system and he could quit stewing about it. But now, on this particular night, it was more like writing something down in order to understand it—to figure it out.

Some of it, the part he was looking forward to thinking about, was opening night. The fact that very soon he would be going onstage in front of hundreds of people, some of whom would have come from many miles away to attend the famous Mannsville 𝕾𝖍𝖆𝖐𝖊𝖘𝖕𝖊𝖆𝖗𝖊 Festival. An audience that would include a lot of critics and reviewers who would write about what they liked and didn't like about this year's production. And the stuff they wrote would then be printed in newspapers all over the state. Maybe even all over the country. Dealing with the fact of opening night was a little nervous making, but at this point mostly just exciting.

But then there was Bernard. The Bernard thing wasn't nearly as pleasant to think about as opening night, but somehow it felt more urgent. Like something that had to be dealt with right away. He didn't know why, except that it would certainly be a relief to be able to believe that Bernard really had changed and would no longer be one more thing to worry about, on opening night or on any of the other nights when William would be too busy being Puck to remember to be on his guard. So, as it turned out, William began his journal entry that night by writing about Bernard Olson. Climbing into bed, he propped himself up with two pillows and began:

> *Well, here I am again writing about something I can't seem to get a handle on, but this time it's a person. This time it's this kid—well, a pretty big kid, who has it in for me because he thought he was for sure going to get to be Puck in*

the Mannsville Shakespeare Festival production of *A Midsummer Night's Dream*, and I got the role instead. So this guy started being very stiff and cold when we happened to meet, and wound up doing things like stealing my promptbook and tearing it up, and putting bacon grease on the rope I use to swing onstage. Which messed up my run-through performance and could have broken my neck.

But then I made the mistake of telling Clarice about it. A really bad mistake, because she decided to tell Bernard that we knew what he'd done. I told her not to, but she did it anyhow. And now, big surprise—Bernard is suddenly acting kind of friendly. I suppose it might be that he's trying to make us think he's sorry for what he did, so we won't tell on him. Like, we might tell Mr. Andre what he did? Except he's probably smart enough to figure out that I haven't any way to prove anything, and people probably would think I just accused him so I didn't have to admit the whole thing just happened because I was showing off or something.

At that point he stopped, remembering how Miss Scott used to say that people who were interested in acting should try to do a lot of their journal writing in the form of dialogue, and then read it over out loud, acting out the parts of the different characters. So when he picked up his pen again, what he started to write was a dialogue between himself and Clarice Ogden. The way it started was:

> One day a guy named William happened to meet a girl he knew—or at least thought he did.

William stopped writing again, wondering if he ought to add something about the fact that this girl was, or at least had been, in love with him. He decided against it.

> That is, he knew who she was and everything, but he didn't _ever_ know what she was going to do next.
>
> _William:_ Hi, Clarice. I want to talk to you.
>
> _Clarice:_ (coldly) Why? What do you want to know?
>
> _William:_ I want to know exactly what you said to Bernard. Because something about him has changed. That's what I want to talk about.
>
> _Clarice:_ (even colder) Okay. Bernard and I are still talking about it. And things have changed. And that's all I have to say about that.

That wasn't word for word the way it had gone, but it was more or less what it meant. So he read it over, making his voice sound as distant and cold as Clarice's had been, and then kind of eagerly interested when he was reading his own part.

He did a good job of it, looking, even feeling, kind of unfriendly and mysteriously secretive when he was being Clarice. But it didn't turn out to be very useful. That is, it didn't prove anything, or even make it easier to understand. Finally he went back to thinking about how great the dress rehearsal had been, and wondering if opening night was going to be that easy—and fun. When he finally turned off the light, he slept all right at first, but then things started happening. Things that seemed too real and vivid to be a dream or even a nightmare.

He was standing in his usual spot in the left wing in his Puck costume, waiting for his prompt, when he looked back and saw a huge, shapeless blob oozing out of the shadows and coming right toward him. He tried to back away, but the blurred image kept getting bigger. As it came closer, he could see huge, billowy arms that seemed to reach out and flow around him. And then, up at the top, an almost human face began to form, a face with mean little eyes and a cruel, sneering grin. Like Rudy's maybe, or one of the twins.

Waking up with a start, William sat straight up and turned on his bedside lamp. Nothing there. No shadows except the ones that came from yesterday's pants and shirt hanging over the back of a chair, and the fainter moving ones that came from the wind-blown curtains. No dark, looming shadows, and no Baggetts! But it was quite a while before his heartbeat slowed down to normal. Turning off the light, he lay back down and pulled the covers over his head.

By the next morning, the morning of opening night, William's mood definitely was having its ups and downs. Or, more accurately, its downs and up, since it certainly started with a downer. It all began as soon as William S. Hardison's eyes began to open, and his half-awake mind suggested that he'd better just go back to sleep, because it wasn't ready to face up to what was about to happen. And what he did next didn't help.

What he did was to stagger out of bed, still half asleep, and cross the room to end up in front of the dresser. He was getting out some underpants when he happened to look at himself in the mirror. To stare at his thin, pointy-chinned face, and his no-particular-colored hair, which at the moment was kind of standing on end, as if he'd just been scared half to death.

What he was looking at was the face of a kid who had been born, not only a "good-for-nothing" Baggett, but also a scrawny, undersized one. And who had the nerve to think that he was about to go on a big stage, in front of hundreds of important people, and make them believe that he was a magical not-quite-human creature known as Robin Goodfellow, or sometimes Puck, a famous character created by **William Shakespeare**, the greatest writer who ever lived.

He leaned closer, hoping to see—he didn't know what. Maybe hoping to see something he'd been missing. Miss Scott said his face was wonderfully expressive, whatever that meant, and once Clarice said he had great eyes. Actually, what she'd said was that he had gorgeous eyes. And it had been Mr. Turner, his dresser and makeup artist, who said he had great cheekbones and an electric smile. But at the moment all he saw when he looked at his face was a skinny, scared-to-death kid.

The fear lasted until he arrived at the cafeteria and sat down with his pancakes and scrambled eggs, and some other members of the cast joined him. Tom/Bottom was one of them, and another was Virginia/Titania, both special friends of his, but there were several others, too. Everyone was talking about how big the audience would be and what important people might be there, but most of them talked to William, too, and said he shouldn't be nervous because he was going to be a big success. They said things like what a natural he was, and how great he'd been in the dress rehearsal, and how everyone thought he was going to steal the show.

By the time breakfast was over, he was feeling a little better. A lot better, really. At least for the time being.

The rest of that long day—the day that would end with opening night of the Mannsville Shakespeare Festival's production of A Midsummer Night's Dream—was an emotional yo-yo for William. Excited anticipation one minute, and absolute panic the next. Panic that came when he let himself imagine stepping out onto the stage and being too stiff with fright to reach for and find the roguish, cocksure creature that Shakespeare had in mind when he wrote about Puck in his midsummer dream play.

The yo-yoing went on—up and down, down and up—right up until the moment that he was standing in the wings in full costume. It wasn't until then that a scared-stiff William Hardison somehow managed a cocky, Puckish grin that seemed to flip a switch and turn it all on. Running his fingers up his pointed elfish ears, he tossed his head and skipped out onto the stage. Forgetting all about the huge crowd on the other side of the proscenium, he became the slightly magical elf who made fun of everything and everybody, except Oberon, king of the fairies, who was his lord and master and told him what to do in no uncertain terms.

It was a familiar, if not entirely controllable transformation, but this time it happened barely in time for act 1, scene 2, where Bottom and Quince were already out on the stage saying silly things about the play they would put on to entertain the duke's wedding guests—and where Mr. Andre had decided that Puck would put in his first appearance. A good decision, because it gave William a chance to ease into his role, by kind of sneaking up on it. By tiptoeing out onstage to duck behind a bush, and then a tree trunk, and peek out as he spied on the would-be actors. And only then, when he'd had a chance to work off any remaining twinges of stage fright, begin to laugh his head off, when Bottom insists he should be the one to play the part of the lion, because he could roar loudly, but at the same time, gently enough so that it wouldn't cause the delicate ladies in the audience to faint.

So when square-headed old Tom Grant opened his toothy mouth very wide and roared and then, like the MGM lion, tipped his shaggy head to one side, the audience laughed. And so did Puck, holding his sides, staggering around, and finally falling down with his legs waving in the air. And the audience laughed even harder.

And then came the beginning of act 2, where the curtain opened on beautiful forest scenery, and where, in Mr. Andre's version of Shakespeare's play, Puck enters by swinging onstage on a vine. As always William had to move quickly while the set was being changed, to get up to the place on the ladder from where, a moment later, he would launch himself out into open space. After scrambling up the narrow ladder, he quickly unhooked the rope, a rope now decorated by plastic leaves and curling tendrils, and without even bothering to sniff for bacon grease, swung out and around and around again, before dropping lightly down, to strut and dance around the stage. The audience obviously liked that a lot too.

Puck's other scenes, the longer speeches as well as the lively acrobatic bits, also seemed to go very well, with lots of applause and bravos. And finally there came the end of act 5, where Puck, all alone on the stage, talks to the audience and says, "'So, good night unto you all. / Give me your hands, if we be friends, / And Robin shall restore amends.'" And the whole audience not only gave him their hands, but also got to their feet and gave a long, loud, standing ovation. And gave another one for every one of the curtain calls he was shoved out to do.

So opening night was over and done with and William had done well. Not only well, but according to what a lot of people were telling him, he had been excellent, sensational, incredible, and a whole lot of other words that he had trouble putting down in his journal, either because they made him feel so self-conscious, or because he wasn't sure how to spell them without looking them up in the dictionary, which he was in no mood to do.

But all the extravagant things that got said, by the important people who came to his dressing room, by everyone at the opening-night cast party, and even by the cooks in the cafeteria—all of it had a "too good to be real" feeling. Not to mention the reviews in the newspapers, even ones from places like Sacramento and San Francisco. Reviews that said people shouldn't miss this year's Mannsville's production because there was a kid in the cast who was an absolute wonder. The whole thing, all of it, had an unreal feeling at times. Exciting and thrilling, of course, but at the same time, confusing. Writing about it in his journal helped William to sort it out a little, but not entirely. There were even times, when the excitement was beginning to dwindle away, when he wrote things like:

> The way I see it, being a big hit onstage is great in most ways, but not so great in a few others. Like for instance, the way people you know feel about what you're doing. Most people seem to think it's swell, but there are some others who don't. Some of my friends have told me that Bernard's father has been putting pressure on Mr. Andre to let Bernard be Puck now and then, maybe every Thursday. So far Mr. Andre says

he can't change the casting. Not while so many
people are coming to the play just to see the Puck
they've been hearing so much about.

So it's pretty easy to see why Bernard, and
his Dean-of-Performing-Arts father, wouldn't
be all that happy about the way things are going.
But they're not the only ones. Like Sydney Apley,
for instance.

Sydney is the tall, good-looking guy who
plays Lysander. He's a real actor who's been in
some other Shakespeare plays, and even a couple
of movies. Tom told me that Sydney has been
saying things about how Mr. Andre is letting me
upstage the whole show.

I know what that means. When an actor
upstages people, he moves to the back of the
stage, which makes the other actors have to turn
their backs on the audience when they talk to
him. I don't have any chance to do that, even if
I wanted to. But upstaging can also mean just
stealing too much attention away from the other
actors, no matter where or how you do it. I guess
I can see what makes Mr. Apley feel the way he
does. After all, he's had a lot more experience
than I have, and he is, for sure and certain, a
whole lot better-looking. But I don't think I'm
upstaging anybody, at least not on purpose.

*And I don't want Sydney, or any of the other
actors, to think I'm trying to.*

William put down his pen and thought for a while
before he went on.

*Another weird thing is the way Clarice has
been acting. I don't know what it is, but I guess
I've really made her mad at me. I mean, she's
just about the only person I know who has never
once said anything to me about how well I've
been doing. Everyone else has, even Bernard,
at least sort of. I don't know what I did, and
I can't find out because she won't talk to me. I
mean, not at all. Like, if I sit down at a table
where she's sitting, she gets up and goes to
another table. It used to be embarrassing when
she sometimes was kind of too friendly, but now
it's embarrassing in the opposite direction.*

*Come to think of it, Clarice isn't the only
thing that's changed a whole lot. Like my whole
life, for instance.*

When he wrote that paragraph about *changes*, William
thought he knew what he meant, but later, when he tried
to make it a little clearer, he found that he didn't know
how. He thought for quite a while about all the ways a

person's life can twist and turn. In his case, how he escaped the Baggetts' tumbledown farmhouse and managed to get himself and the other kids to his aunt's house, but then Big Ed and two of his gigantic kids turned up again and dragged them back. Back to where William had to take the blame, and a lot of punishment, before all four of them finally—and legally—got rescued. And then, when he had barely gotten used to being a Hardison, he had the chance to become—Puck. A pretty successful and, you might even say, famous Puck. That was a whole lot of twists and turns for a life to take in not quite fourteen years. And now, finally, a life that had started out looking pretty hopeless had become . . . a dream come true? Yes, that's for sure. But a life that, even so, still seemed to be coming up with some unexpected ups and downs.

At last he decided he just wasn't going to be able to put it into words that meant anything, at least not without a lot more time to think about it. Maybe he'd be able to someday, but in the meantime he would just go to bed and sleep on it.

So July slipped by, with day after day of Mannsville's famous good weather, and even more famous Shakespearean production, and then suddenly it was mid-August, and closing night was only a couple of weeks away. The audiences had stayed big and enthusiastic, and all sorts of people were still telling William that he was a marvelous Puck, and that he had a great career as an actor ahead of him, and a lot of other stuff that he was beginning to be able to listen to without feeling too embarrassed to enjoy it. That, in particular, was one change that had happened slowly.

There were some things, however, that didn't seem to have changed all that much since the summer began—William's height, for instance, and his lack of any really impressive muscles. As well as the fact that, while his face seemed to be the type for not-quite-human roles like Puck and Ariel, it still wasn't about to remind anyone of Gary Cooper or Cary Grant.

Of course, it was a dream come true to be at Mannsville

and have an important role in one of their Shakespeare festival productions. Even when he wasn't onstage being cheered and clapped for, there were a lot of good times, making new friends and learning how to talk to important people such as newspaper reporters and drama critics. And talking and making jokes with old friends like Tom and Virginia and, of course, Miss Scott and Mr. Andre. As well as people like Sergeant Blanding, the campus policeman whose beat included the theater on performance nights. Sergeant Blanding was an enormous man with a loud laugh, who liked to tell William that he was his biggest fan, and then add, "Really big, all two hundred and sixty pounds of me."

It definitely was the best summer of William's entire life—one he knew he would never forget. But that didn't mean he couldn't find some things to worry about when he woke up in the middle of the night.

One problem that changed back and forth but never really went away was Clarice. She still wouldn't talk to him at all. He tried for a while, but when her clenched teeth and slit-eyed glare got to be almost as embarrassing as her Helena and Demetrius act had been, he more or less quit trying.

And as for Bernard, he seemed to have changed too. Strangely enough, he went on being almost friendly. At least he smiled stiffly now and then and said hi. But he never said much, and nothing at all, to William at least, about being his understudy. Not anymore. As the summer went by, Bernard was still around quite a bit, hanging out backstage or in the greenroom, even though everybody knew that the only role he was playing now was "the privileged son of the super-important Dean Olson of Mannsville College's performing arts department."

It was on a Wednesday in mid-August when an envelope with William's name on it appeared on the call-board in the greenroom. There was something familiar about the handwriting, and sure enough, when he opened it he found it was from Miss Scott. A short note that only said that she would like to see him in her office tomorrow, at ten o'clock in the morning.

Miss Scott's office was a small room in a building not far from the theater, and when William got there she was putting some papers away in a filing cabinet. She turned to smile at him and say, "And here you are, right on time. Please sit down. I'll be with you in a minute."

So William sat down and got out a pencil and his new promptbook, in case she wanted to suggest some new stage business. But after she finished with the filing, she sat down at her desk and stared at him for a long minute before she said, "Just look at you, William. When I do, what I can't help seeing is Mannsville's biggest success story of 1939. And of course, I'm very pleased. But, you know, I sometimes think that I, and the rest of the staff, should be thinking a bit more about the problems you may have to cope with because of what this summer has done to your life."

She was smiling, so he smiled back, but behind the smile he was feeling confused and more than a little embarrassed. What was she talking about?

She went on, "Here you are. A kid who's just barely teenage, and who comes from a . . . well, you might say . . ." She rolled her eyes and shrugged. "A difficult background?"

"A disgusting background," William said, grinning. "Very *disgusting!*"

She laughed. "Well, all right. Whatever you want to call it. Of course—"

But at that point William couldn't help interrupting. "They don't know, do they? I mean, Mr. Andre and everybody? Do they know all about the Baggetts and everything?"

Miss Scott shook her head. "No," she said. "I've told them about your Ariel role, of course, but that's about it. And I'm sure Clarice hasn't said anything about that part of your background either. She promised me she wouldn't. But regardless of your background, people here have been amazed and surprised at your seemingly inborn talent."

Feeling his face getting warm, William ducked his head.

"You surprised everyone, even me," she went on. "That

is, I knew of course, after your Ariel role, that you had a lot of natural ability, but I didn't foresee the kind of success you've had here at Mannsville. And it has occurred to me lately that such a sudden transformation in your life might be . . ."

She paused, smiling slightly before she went on, "I've heard about other young people who received early and seemingly easy success, who weren't able to handle it very well. The thing is, William, I do so hope this summer's acclaim hasn't changed you too much."

William grinned and, sticking out his arms and legs, pretended to look himself over carefully. "'Fraid not. Looks like the same old scarecrow to me."

Miss Scott laughed. "As much of a natural clown as ever, too. And I hope just as brave and patient." She paused before she nodded and went on. "I mean, you still have several years of school ahead of you, along with helping your aunt raise her big new family. And I'm afraid not all of your immediate future is going to be anywhere near as grand and glorious as this summer has been."

For a long moment William went on fiddling with his pencil before he looked up, raised an eyebrow, and said, "You mean you think I might just chuck it all and run off to Hollywood. Or something like that?"

She laughed. "Something like that."

"I know." He nodded. "I know what you mean. I've thought about it. About what it's going to be like, going back to Gold Beach." He grinned ruefully. "To a high school that doesn't even have a drama department."

"And?" Miss Scott asked.

He gave her a Puckish grin. "I think I can deal with it."

Miss Scott nodded slowly as she said, "Yes, I think you can too."

After that they only talked about fairly normal things like the weather and the sneezing fit little old Jerry, the changeling, had on stage the other night, and how it had cracked up the audience. And what the weather might be like for closing night. And then Miss Scott thanked him for stopping by and said she wanted him to keep in touch when he was back in Gold Beach. And that was about all there was to it.

But later, when William had had time to think about what Miss Scott had said, he did wonder about some of the things she'd brought up. He didn't think she needed to worry about the patience thing, though. Growing up as an undersized Baggett, patience was one thing you had to have a lot of.

But Miss Scott had been wrong about bravery. Apparently she had somehow gotten the idea that he was brave. *Bad guess*, William thought. For instance, if he'd been brave, he wouldn't have been so patient about being a Baggett. Jancy had been the brave one. She was the one who had decided it was time to pack up and make a run for it.

Remembering the escape brought it all back. Brought back why and how the four youngest Baggetts had managed to set off in the dead of night—how they were hidden for so long in the Ogdens' basement, how they finally made it to their aunt's house, and had been safe and happy briefly, before they were kidnapped back again by the Baggetts. And then, at long last, being rescued by Miss Scott and Clarice's lawyer parents, who got rid of the Baggetts for good and always. At least got rid of them legally, and in William's case at least, when he was wide awake. He shrugged, telling himself to forget those scary Baggett dreams. *Dreams don't count,* he told himself. *What counts is what happens when you're wide awake.*

But somehow, remembering some of those hard times after so many days, weeks even, of thinking only about what a famous Puck he'd become, made William feel . . . well, a little guilty, but also really eager to see them again—all four of them. Easygoing Aunt Fiona, brave, tough Jancy, and too-cute-for-her-own-good Trixie. And Buddy? As for hardheaded, hard-sleeping, little old Buddy who had been William's special responsibility and pain in the neck for so long? Somehow it seemed to William that most of all, he was looking forward to seeing Buddy again.

He checked the calendar. August 14. If everything went well, like Aunt Fiona being able to get her brakes fixed, it would be not quite two weeks until all the Hardisons arrived in Mannsville. Okay, he told himself. Brave or not, patient or not, Miss Scott needn't worry about him forgetting his family. He, William 𝔖. Hardison, really was looking forward to the day when he'd be back in Gold Beach, whether it was as a slightly famous 𝔖𝔥𝔞𝔨𝔢𝔰𝔭𝔢𝔞𝔯𝔢𝔞𝔫 actor, or as nothing more than an ordinary freshman at a high school that didn't even have a drama department.

So that was what William decided on August 14, and it was the very next day when he received a letter from Jancy. A letter from Jancy Hardison, with another one from Aunt Fiona tucked into the same envelope.

Jancy's letter began:

> It's for sure now that we are all coming. Buddy and I happened to run into Mr. Fisher in the grocery store. You remember, he's the nice guy who let us ride in his rumble seat? And Buddy talked him into fixing Aunt Fiona's brakes for free. So now Aunt Fiona has written to Miss Scott and asked her to find a motel in Mannsville that doesn't cost too much. So we'll all be coming for a couple of days. And after closing night we can all ride home together. Isn't that swell? I can hardly wait.
>
> Somebody sent Aunt Fiona a clipping from the _Crownfield Daily_ that told about what a big success you are in _A Midsummer Night's_

<u>Dream</u>. And Aunt Fiona sent it to the <u>Gold Beach Independent</u>, and they printed it too. And Aunt Fiona's friends keep calling her to tell her that they heard about what you are doing. Just about everyone in Gold Beach seems to know about you. Yesterday in the grocery store your friend Charlie Bowen talked and talked to me about how famous you are, and how much fun it was when you guys used to practice acrobatics in his barn.

But I still just wish you were home right now. Everything goes better when you are here. Especially Buddy. Like, last night he and Trixie had a fight over the last piece of pie. Trixie said she ought to have it because she was older and prettier. So Buddy gave her a shove and said he was going to get it because he was bigger and meaner. What he said word for word, was, "Prettier doesn't count. Bigger and meaner is what gets the pie."

That's exactly what he said, William. Bigger and meaner is what gets the pie.

And Aunt Fiona just laughed and hugged him and said he wasn't mean enough to scare her. That's the way she is about Buddy. I think it must be because she had him first when he was a helpless little newborn baby, and she just can't *see that he's not all that helpless anymore. It really worries me, William.*

*But, anyway, you'll see us soon. All of us, the pretty ones and the mean ones—and me.*

Jancy

Aunt Fiona's letter was much shorter. She just said how delighted she was that they would be able to see him in 𝕬 𝔐idsummer 𝔑ight's 𝔇ream. And how it wouldn't be long now.

No, it wouldn't be, William thought, as he got ready for bed. Not long until he was back in Gold Beach with all of them and, as Miss Scott had pointed out, no more big cheering audiences and standing ovations, and autograph signing. Instead there would just be school, and being at home with Aunt Fiona and Jancy and the kids.

And could Buddy really be turning into a typical Baggett? William sighed and pulled the covers over his head.

## CHAPTER 20

The next morning William checked off another day on his calendar. Four more performances this week, two nights off on Monday and Tuesday, and then the last week of 𝕸𝖎𝖉𝖘𝖚𝖒𝖒𝖊𝖗 would start, and his family would be arriving. He found himself thinking about it quite a lot, and even bringing it up in the greenroom and cafeteria, when anyone seemed interested. Both Virginia and Tom had a lot to say about how great they thought it was that his family was finally going to get to see for themselves what a smashing job he was doing in an important 𝕾𝖍𝖆𝖐𝖊𝖘𝖕𝖊𝖆𝖗𝖊𝖆𝖓 production.

It was at breakfast on Wednesday morning that Tom said, "And we're going to get to meet them, aren't we? Can't wait. However, I can't help wondering . . . Aren't the two little ones a bit young to sit still for two hours of Shakespeare?"

William assured him they'd be fine. "They can practically recite the play by heart, and 𝕿𝖍𝖊 𝕿𝖊𝖒𝖕𝖊𝖘𝖙, too. All last year when I was practicing I used to try to make them line up and sit still and listen while I did my speeches." He grinned. "Sometimes they did, but Jancy and her guinea pig were the only audience I could always count on."

"Aha." Tom waggled his finger in the air. Looking around at the other people at the table, he said, "So that's his secret. All you have to do is to round up some toddlers and a guinea pig to critique your rehearsals, and you'll soon be stealing the show, like our young friend here." Everyone laughed, and William did too, but behind the laughter, that stuff about "stealing the show" made him a little uneasy.

He was still thinking about the "stealing the show" remark when he got to the greenroom that afternoon. Thinking and wishing that there was something he could say to people like Sydney Apley, for instance, so that they'd know he wasn't doing it on purpose. But then, as he walked into the crowded room, something happened that took his mind off the "show stealing" problem.

He was barely inside the room when he noticed that Clarice was coming toward him, smiling a big smile and batting her eyes the way she used to before she got mad at him. But then, just as he was beginning to smile back, she went right past him. So William went on until he reached the other side of the room, where he turned around and saw that the person Clarice had been smiling at had been—Bernard. Bernard?

And now the two of them were talking as they walked toward the coffee bar. Or at least Clarice was, talking and smiling, and Bernard seemed to be listening. She went on until they came to the refrigerator, where they stopped long enough for Bernard to start getting out some Cokes. At that point William decided he needed to check the call-board and went in the other direction.

Nothing new on the call-board, but he stood there for a while reading old notices while he thought over what he had just seen and what it meant. And what, if anything, he ought to do about it. Perhaps it was because he'd been worrying about what Tom had said about "stealing the show," or for some other reason, but William had been having a vague feeling that he ought to apologize to someone. And now it occurred to him that maybe he should apologize to Clarice, for whatever he'd done that had made her so mad at him. Or else to Bernard for . . . for what?

He'd gotten about that far when Mr. Turner, his dresser, came by and said, "Hey, there you are, Mr. Goodfellow." He pointed to his watch. "Time to suit up."

So then came another performance with another full house and, as usual, lots of clapping and cheering for William during his curtain calls. It wasn't until later, when he was back in his room in the dormitory, that he had time to think some more about seeing Clarice and Bernard in the greenroom. It was kind of confusing. So much so that he decided he should try to write about it, to see if that might help him to figure it out. So he got out his journal and began.

So—I saw something this afternoon that's kind of hard to make heads or tails of. Clarice and Bernard talking together. Or at least Bernard listening while Clarice talked to him—in a very friendly way. The thing is, back when she was still speaking to me, she was insisting that we should tell everybody that Bernard stole my promptbook and greased my entry rope. She kept insisting that we should tell on him because he ought to be punished for what he did. And the very last time she talked to me, she said she'd already told him that we knew what he did. So he knows, and that might explain why he's trying to be friendlier, so I might forgive him and not tell on him. But that doesn't explain why Clarice stopped speaking to me. Stopped absolutely. I mean not even hi. All I can think is, maybe she's trying to make him think she's his friend and not mine so he'll confess. Or else he's sorry for what he did, and she's forgiven him. Or else I just don't understand females.

That night William put his journal away, thinking he would come up with some more ideas on the subject of Clarice and Bernard in the next day or two. But there was so much else to do, and so many people to talk to, that he hadn't gotten around to it when he woke up one morning and it was Friday, and his family was due to arrive in Mannsville that very afternoon.

The day dragged by, and as it got closer and closer to the time that they might be arriving, William went down to sit in the lounge of Edwin Hall near the receptionist's desk, so he could get to the phone in a hurry. It was a good thing he'd brought a book with him, because it wasn't until almost five o'clock that the phone rang, and when Mrs. Rogers, the receptionist, picked it up, she motioned for William to come. "It's for you," she said with a big smile. "They're here."

It was Aunt Fiona on the phone, and after they'd said hello she told him that they had checked into their motel to freshen up, and they were ready to drive to the college campus. "And where shall we meet you?" Aunt Fiona wanted to know. In the background a familiar voice was saying, "Here, let me. I want to talk to Willum."

William looked at his watch. "Well," he told Aunt Fiona, "I have to be at the theater by seven, so I don't know if I'll have time to go downtown for dinner."

"I know," Aunt Fiona said. "You won't need to. Miss Scott sent me a map of Mannsville and a complimentary pass to the cafeteria for the whole family, as well as tickets to tonight's performance. If you can just tell me how to get to Edwin Hall, we'll come pick you up, and we can all go to the cafeteria together." And then not exactly into the phone, but loud enough for William to hear, "All right. *All right*, Buddy. But not for long. Just say hello."

There was a pause and then a *whack* and a *clackety-clack* noise, as if the phone had been dropped and picked up again, and then Buddy's growly little voice was saying, "Hi, Willum. We're in a motel. Where are *you*?"

"Hi, Buddy. I'm at Edwin Hall. It's a big dormitory. You're going to come meet me here."

"What's a doritory?" Buddy said. "Is it a long way? We already came a long way. We're hungry. There's nothing in a motel but beds and a baffroom. Nothing to eat. Willum, what I want is—"

But then Aunt Fiona was saying, "Here, Buddy. Give me the phone, please. No, no. Give it to me. Right *now*, Buddy."

After that there were some more scuffling noises, and then Aunt Fiona came on again and William was able to tell her how to get to Edwin Hall. Outside the dormitory's double doors, William sat down on the top step to wait.

hen Aunt Fiona's old blue Dodge pulled up in front of Edwin Hall, all three of the kids jumped out and ran up the steps. Watching them come, William noticed that Jancy's thick, curly hair looked like a real hairdo now, instead of a mop, and that Trixie still looked a lot like Shirley Temple. And as for Buddy . . . He was still kind of big for his age. Nothing new about that, except that now his big grin exposed one thing that was new and different. A gap where one of his front teeth used to be.

William had just started down the stairs when they were all over him. Grabbing his hands and hugging him and talking a mile a minute, except for Buddy, who just stood there and grinned until William poked him in the chest and asked, "You losing your teeth already, kid?"

"I didn't lose it," Buddy said proudly. "It's right here in my pocket. It got knocked out." His grin widened. "I knocked out two of his."

But then Trixie interrupted by hanging on to William's

arm as she bounced up onto her tiptoes and down again. "Here we are. Look at me, William. I have a new dress. See my new dress, William?"

"Hey," Jancy was saying, "you said you hadn't grown any, but I think you have. You look bigger, William. Taller and everything." She looked up at Edwin Hall. "Wow. Is this where you live? It's huge. Look, kids. This is where William lives. Right here in this great big building."

"Is it a palace?" Trixie said. "Can we see it? I want to see." She ran up and opened one of the double doors and peeked in. "Oh look, Jancy," she said. "It's *so* big."

So they all had to peek in with Trixie saying, "Where's your bed, William? Where do you sleep?"

And Buddy asking, "Where's the kitchen?"

By then Aunt Fiona was there too, hugging William and asking him how much time he had before he had to report to the theater.

"Oh, there's time," he told her. "I don't have to be there till seven, and it isn't far to the cafeteria. If we go in the car, it will only take a couple of minutes. Come on. I'll show you my room."

So he led the way up to room 217 and showed them where he slept, and the great view from his window, before they took off for the cafeteria. William was right about how quickly they could get there, but what he hadn't foreseen was that it was going to take longer than usual to get through the line. All the cooks came out of the kitchen to say hello and shake hands, and laugh when Buddy insisted that William lift him up over the counter so he could be sure he'd gotten some of everything—except the string beans. And even after they all had their food and were seated at a table, they were still the center of attention. Other members of the cast and crew kept coming over to be introduced, and to say things about what a great job William was doing, and that he was the big hit of the show, and other friendly, if slightly embarrassing, things.

But when the crowd was thinning out and the members of the cast were all leaving for the theater, Buddy was still eating. William took out his map of the campus and showed Aunt Fiona how to get to the theater. "And you don't have to be there right away," he told her. "But the doors open at seven thirty. Just be sure you get there pretty soon after that. If you see a big, tall man in a blue uniform, that's Sergeant Blanding. He's a friend of mine, and he said he'd show you a good place to park."

Taking the map, Aunt Fiona said, "It looks like quite a ways. Don't you want me to drive you?"

"Oh no," William said. "I'm used to it. I'll probably catch a ride, and even if I don't, I can run there in ten minutes."

So he was off at a trot, and only a few minutes later he was in his dressing room, telling his dresser about his family and how they would be in the audience tonight, while he was helped into his tights and tunic, and got his pointed elf ears taped on.

It wasn't until Mr. Turner had finished with him and—elf-eared, face painted, and dressed in his leafy tunic—he was on his way through the dimly lit wings, that he realized that the special excitement he'd been feeling had faded away, leaving behind an uneasy premonition that something was about to happen. Something strange and threatening. Bernard again? Up to some other nasty trick? He stopped and looked around. Nothing. No sign of Bernard or anything out of the ordinary that he might have done. Just a lot of hanging curtains and cardboard sets, and in between only the usual dimly lit spaces.

Moving on, William told himself that what he was feeling wasn't at all the same as the stage fright he'd had when he was waiting for his audition, or for his cue on opening night. This was different.

He had stopped two or three times before he suddenly figured it out. It was just the memory of that stupid dream. The one about the shapeless shadow that had oozed out of the backstage darkness and turned into something that looked almost like a Baggett.

He shrugged and grinned ruefully, telling himself to forget it. "It was just a stupid dream," he whispered. "Only a dream."

At that moment his entry cue pushed everything else out of his mind. Tiptoeing out onto the stage, hiding behind trees and bushes, he spied on Quince and Bottom and, as easily as ever, turned into the acrobatic, mischievous Robin Goodfellow, servant of King Oberon.

The show went as usual, with the audience laughing along with Puck while he overheard the villagers planning their play, and gasping and then clapping as he made his acrobatic entry, on a vine that didn't feel or smell like bacon grease.

Entirely forgetting, at least for the time being, his strange attack of nervousness, he threw himself into the role as completely as ever, or even more so. Once or twice during his longer speeches—remembering how, when he was practicing back home, he sometimes had to poke Trixie or Buddy to wake them up—he threw in a bit of extra action like a backward flip or a handstand, just to liven things up a bit.

And then, at last, it was time for the final curtain and, as usual, Puck got the loudest applause and the most curtain calls. And afterward his family came into his dressing room, bouncing and bubbling with excitement.

Aunt Fiona wanted to know who had decided to pad Puck's part so much. She was smiling as she said, "An amazing performance, William. But tell me something. I've seen this play before, more than once, and I don't recall seeing all that much of our friend Robin Goodfellow."

"I know." William grinned. "It happened kind of gradually. The director just kept thinking of other business for me to do. So I'd try it out, and if he liked it he'd put it in for good. Oh, once in a while he'd say just forget it, but a lot of the time he told me to keep doing it."

Jancy just kept saying "wonderful," in a voice that absolutely quivered with enthusiasm. "It was so wonderful. You were wonderful, William. Everything was wonderful. Wonderful."

Trixie said she thought William was wonderful too, but if she was ever in **A Midsummer Night's Dream** she would rather be a fairy, because their costumes were prettier.

And Buddy grinned his gap-toothed grin and said, "I mostly liked it too. Most of the time I didn't sleep very much."

As soon as William got out of his costume, he took the whole family around backstage. They visited the greenroom and the costume room and met all the backstage crew. Jerry and some of the younger fairies had already gone home, but two of the older ones were still there. The one named Alicia let Trixie try on her wings, which caused a long delay when Trixie refused to take them off until she had admired herself in every mirror in the costume room.

It was very late when they left the auditorium, and the parking lot had pretty much emptied except for Sergeant Blanding and an old woman who was having trouble starting her enormous Cadillac. The whole family walked out into the parking lot just in time to see the big policeman single-handedly push the Cadillac halfway across the lot until the motor caught and it finally started.

They were all very impressed. Especially Buddy. When they finally got into the Dodge and headed for Edwin Hall, and the rest of them went back to talking about William and **Shakespeare**, Buddy went on talking about how that policeman pushed that great big car all by himself.

## CHAPTER 22

That night, when he was finally back in Edwin Hall, William fell asleep as soon as his head hit the pillow, so it wasn't until much later that he woke up remembering the strange feeling that he'd had just before he went onstage. Coming suddenly back to consciousness out of a deep sleep, he was once more aware of the premonition that something unpleasant was close, and getting closer. He tossed and turned for what seemed like a long time, reminding himself over and over again that it had just been a silly dream, before he finally was able to go back to sleep.

The next morning at breakfast everything seemed pretty normal. The two littlest Hardisons were full of eager excitement and, just as before, lots of the cast came over to their table to visit. Even Sydney Apley, who wasn't a particular friend of William's, came over to test the rumor that Trixie and Buddy knew the names of all the characters in the play and could pick out who played each part. When Sydney asked them if they knew who he was, Trixie and Buddy both said, "Lysander" or, in Buddy's case, something pretty close to it.

"I know. I know," Buddy shouted. "You're Landslider. You're the one William hits in the eye with the flower."

Even Clarice came over to the table and chatted with Aunt Fiona and the kids, and though she didn't actually talk to William, she didn't glare at him as much as usual. And when he said hi, she even went, "Hi" back in a fairly polite tone of voice. But after she left, Jancy scooted her chair closer to William, and when everyone else was busy talking to Trixie and Buddy, she whispered, "She's mad at you, isn't she? Clarice is mad at you."

William grinned. "Oh really?" he asked. "How did you guess?"

Jancy frowned thoughtfully. "Why is she? What did you do?"

William shook his head. "Who knows?" he told Jancy. "I sure don't. I'd ask her if she'd talk to me."

Jancy's nod was quick and firm. "I'll find out."

William only shrugged, but what he was thinking was, *Good luck.*

It wasn't until the crowd had pretty much thinned out that William and Aunt Fiona had time to make some plans for the rest of the day. After breakfast they would all spend some time in downtown Mannsville and then go for a swim in the college's swimming pool. That caused a lot of enthusiasm, because there wasn't anywhere to swim in Gold Beach, except the Pacific Ocean. And then Trixie and Buddy got into an argument about whether a swimming pool was better than an ocean.

Trixie preferred swimming pools because all that sand was so messy, but Buddy said messy didn't matter. "Oceans are bigger, and big is what matters." The argument went on until William interrupted everybody to remind them that when the day was over, "Then comes closing night, and my very last performance as Puck."

Everyone at the table turned to look at him, and Jancy said what all of them must have been thinking. "Will you be sad?" she asked. "Will you be sorry it's over?"

He thought for a moment before he said, "I guess I will. Sort of." He grinned at Buddy. "Except for the ears. I won't miss those ears."

"Why?" Trixie wanted to know. "I like the way those ears look." She cocked her head and made pointed ears out of her hands.

"Yeah. I guess they look pretty Puckish," he said. "But the tape that holds them on gets tangled up in my hair, and after a while it starts to hurt." He shrugged and grinned. "I'll bet fairy wings would get uncomfortable too, if you wore them long enough."

Getting back to making plans for the day, William let the kids know they didn't have to sit through the play again if they didn't want to. "If you've had all the Shakespeare you can take for now, we could—"

"Could what?" Buddy demanded.

"Well, I don't know," William said. "Maybe Jancy could . . ." He started to say "babysit," and decided against it. "Maybe Jancy could stay at the motel with you and just Aunt Fiona could go to the play again, or—"

"But I want to go again. I really, really want to, William," Jancy said.

"So, how about it? Could you see the play one more time?" Aunt Fiona asked, and Trixie and Buddy agreed, if not too enthusiastically.

"Okay, okay. If I can go see the fairies again afterward," Trixie finally said.

So then William had to tell her that she couldn't, because there was to be a closing-night party for just the cast and crew right after the final curtain. "It's kind of a Mannsville tradition, and no one is invited except the people in the play," William told her. "It's a strict rule on closing night. And we're not supposed to have any dressing room visitors tonight either, so the cast can get together in the greenroom right after the final curtain. Okay?" Trixie pouted for a while but she finally said okay.

So that was the way they left it. The Hardison family would all sit—or sleep—through A Midsummer Night's Dream one more time, and then Aunt Fiona would take them back to the motel so William would be free to go to the closing-night party. And the next morning, just like the day before, they'd meet William at the cafeteria.

Then they'd stop by Edwin Hall just long enough to pick up his suitcase before they started off on the long trip back to Gold Beach.

That was the plan, anyway, and everything seemed to be going along smoothly, right through until the final curtain. A curtain with even more applause and standing ovations than usual. And William's response, his bows and kisses thrown to the audience, seemed different too, because even as he bowed and waved, he was suddenly very much aware that his life as Robin Goodfellow was about to end. To end completely, as was his existence as an actor who was praised and applauded night after night, and followed around by people wanting to have him autograph their programs.

And so, what would come next? That wasn't a question he'd given much thought to until that night. Always before he'd taken all those curtain calls still feeling like the sassy, quick-witted servant of King Oberon. There just hadn't been any time to worry about what the future would hold for William "ex-Baggett" Hardison. But that night, as the final curtain came down, and even while the cheers and clapping were still going on, he was suddenly very much aware that this was the end.

By the time he was finally able to head for his dressing room, he was struggling with a throat-tightening, eye-flooding surge of emotions. He'd only meant to stop off in his dressing room long enough to get rid of his uncomfortable ears. But once there he was glad for the chance to wipe his eyes and get control of himself before he headed for the greenroom.

So, taking his time, he worked slowly and deliberately as he pulled at the painfully sticky tape. He was still wincing from detaching the second ear, when something happened that took his mind completely off sad endings, and painful elf ears as well.

It began with some hurried footsteps just outside his dressing room door, an unexpected sound that caused him to turn away from the mirror in time to see the door open and Buddy stomp into the room.

"Buddy!" William yelped impatiently. "What are you doing here? Didn't you hear me say I have to go to a party that's only for people in the play? Where's Aunt Fiona? You're supposed to go back to the motel with—"

He hadn't even finished his sentence when Buddy shook his head fiercely and squealed, "I know. I know that. I was going to, but then I saw them. I saw some Baggetts."

"You saw *what?*"

"Baggetts. Two of them."

William didn't believe it. He desperately didn't want to believe it. "Where?" He gasped. "Where did you see them? Buddy, you couldn't have seen Baggetts."

Buddy nodded hard. "I did too. I did too see them."

"Did Aunt Fiona and Jancy see them?"

Buddy shook his head. "I don't think so. Aunt Fiona and Jancy and Trixie were all in the ladies' baffroom. I saw them all by myself. I saw Rudy, and Gary, too. They didn't see me, I think, maybe. So I ran real fast to tell you."

Even as a sudden memory of last night's scary premonition pushed its way into his mind, William went on trying to convince himself it couldn't be true. What would Baggetts be doing so far away from Crownfield, and at a play by 𝔚𝔦𝔩𝔩𝔦𝔞𝔪 𝔖𝔥𝔞𝔨𝔢𝔰𝔭𝔢𝔞𝔯𝔢? It just wasn't possible. "Are you sure that's who you saw? You haven't seen them for more than a year. They must have changed since then."

"They did." Buddy nodded. "They got bigger. But they're still Baggetts. Both of them."

William shook his head, and went on shaking it, telling himself that Buddy must have been mistaken, but at the same time, being more and more afraid he hadn't. And if Buddy was right, what should he, William, do about it? The first thing that came to mind was that he had to get Buddy safely back to Aunt Fiona.

"Does Aunt Fiona know where you are?" he asked.

Buddy shook his head. "No. I told you. She was still in the ladies' baffroom. I ran too fast to wait and tell her."

William had been afraid of that. And by now she was probably really worried about where he'd gotten to. "Well, come on," he told Buddy. "The first thing we have to do is take you back to—"

But at that very moment the dressing room door opened again and two big men pushed their way into the room. Like Buddy said, they were even bigger, but they were Rudy and Gary Baggett, all right. No doubt about that.

## CHAPTER 23

They were grinning. Rudy's big whiskery chin and Gary's lumpy face were both stretched into what was probably supposed to look like smiles as they tried to shove all four of their big shoulders through the doorway at the same time. Once inside, they both turned and slammed the door shut behind them. Slammed it hard. Then for a minute they just stood there, grinning at William as he backed away across the dressing room.

It was Rudy who spoke first. "Well, well, well," he said. "It's him all right. Jus' like we heard. Our skinny little brother making himself famous by prancin' around in front of hundreds and hundreds and hundreds of people. I cain't hardly believe it, Gary. Can you?"

Gary shook his head. "No siree," he said. "Cain't hardly. But it's him all right, underneath all that face paint. We seen it with our own eyes, just like Pa told us we had to, just to be sure, before we done anything about it. Pa heard about it and even saw it in the papers, but he just couldn't believe it really was our own little Willy."

"Right you are," Rudy said. "And don't think we ain't proud of you. Getting to be a famous person at your age." He threw back his head and laughed loudly. "And we feel pretty lucky, don't we, Gary? Not everybody gets to have a rich and famous person for a little brother. Ain't that right, Gary?"

It wasn't until then, backed up against the dressing room mirror, that William began to understand why a couple of Baggetts had spent the evening watching **Shakespeare**. To understand, and fear the worst. Catching his breath and swallowing hard, he said, "Now, wait a minute. Just a minute. I'm not your brother. Not any longer. I'm a legal Hardison now. All four of us are. And I'm—"

Gary came closer, with Rudy right behind him. "That don't mean nothing, and you know it." Gary's voice was turning into a typical Baggetty growl. "It's blood that counts, and by blood you're a Baggett and you always will be."

Rudy grabbed Gary's shoulder and pulled him back. "Now, hold on there, Bub," he said to Gary. "We don't want to cause no trouble or hurt nobody. Not unless we have to, that is." As he turned back to William, his phony smile was changing into a sad-eyed plea. "It's just that Pa's been real bad lately, his bad back and all. He's been out of work mostly all last year. All of us have been. And his relief money got cut a lot since the four of you skipped out on us. What Pa's been thinking is that you might see fit to help out a little with some of this playactin' gold mine you fell into. I mean, seeing as how we're still your rightful kin and always will be."

His voice went on and on, but William didn't have to hear any more to know what was happening and why. They had come to ask for, to demand, money. A lot of it. And he also knew that, given what they'd read in the papers and maybe even heard on the radio about what a hit he had been, they'd never believe him when he told them he hadn't made any money. They'd never believe him, but it was the truth, and he would try to tell them so. He'd see if he could make them understand, but before he started, he had to think of some way to get Buddy out of the room. To be sure they wouldn't have a chance to take it out on Buddy, if they didn't believe him. Backed up against the mirror, William looked around quickly—and then looked again more carefully. No Buddy, anywhere.

Where could he have gone? Not under the makeup counter or behind the chair. There were no other shelves or cupboards big enough to hide a five-year-old as substantial as Buddy. But then William realized what must have happened. The door that Rudy had slammed so hard was now not quite shut. It looked as if Buddy must have scooted behind them when they were walking across the room, and while they were yelling he must have quietly opened the door and slipped out.

*Good for you, Buddy,* William was thinking, when he felt Rudy's big hand on his shoulder and stopped thinking of anything except how he could make the two of them believe the truth. The truth that except for a little change in his pocket, he had no money at all.

"Listen. Please listen," he began. "Here at Mannsville, beginning actors who aren't members of Actors' Equity or anything don't get paid except just their room and board. See, when an amateur auditions and gets a role here, it's considered just a part of their training and they don't get any real pay." He could tell his voice was shaky and unconvincing, but he kept trying. "The thing is, I don't have any money at all."

One of Rudy's big hands was moving from William's shoulder up to his throat. "Don't give me that, kid," he said. "We saw how you got more cheerin' and clappin' than any of them other dudes. Don't try to tell me the big shots who run this place don't know what side their bread's buttered on. They pay crowd-pleasers like you a bundle. They got to, or some other show-business guy comes along and hires their big star away, and pays 'em even more. That's what Pa says, and you know it's the truth, and don't think for a minute that we're too dumb to figure it out." His fingers tightened. "Now, where's our part?"

It went on and on for what seemed like forever, with William trying to pull Rudy's fingers off his throat, while both of them yelled at him. First one and then the other, or sometimes both of them at once, saying things like, "Big Ed says just a couple of hundred bucks would do, at least for right now. Just enough to help us pay a few bills." And then, "Our old man knew you'd try to lie to us, like saying you ain't got paid yet, or some such baloney. He warned us about believing any of your smart-mouth lies. He says nobody gets their faces and names in all those newspapers unless he got bushels of money already."

William was still struggling, trying to talk, trying to make them believe the truth. But Rudy's big fingers were still on his throat when the dressing room door opened again, with a loud bang. Rudy's grip tightened as he whirled around, dragging William with him. Before his mind went blank, William heard a deep voice shouting, "Okay. What is this? What's going on here?" And another voice, high-pitched and squeaky, saying, "Stop. Stop that. Make them stop, Sergeant."

And then William was thrown against the wall like a rag doll, and everything went dark and blank. But it couldn't have been much more than a few seconds later that he began to be aware that he was sitting on a chair with Sergeant Blanding bending over him, and no Baggetts anywhere in sight. Groggy as he was, he managed to make sure of that.

"You all right, kid?" The sergeant was holding him upright and patting his cheek. "How you doing, boy?

How about a little sip of water? Get that glass, Buddy. Over there on the table."

Still feeling too limp to turn his head, William only rolled his eyes to watch Buddy scoot off to get the glass, carefully fill it at the tap, trot back, trip—and spill most of it in William's lap. That did it. Suddenly William Hardison was fully conscious and feeling pretty much back to normal, except for being a little bit soggy. He was even grinning a little as he told the policeman where to find a towel.

And not much later Sergeant Blanding saw William to the door of the greenroom, before he headed off to find Aunt Fiona, carrying Buddy on his shoulders. But before he left he told William, "I'll be back to get you in *one hour*. No later." He motioned toward the door of the greenroom, where the cast party was already going full blast. "That bunch will probably be carryin' on till daybreak, but it seems to me you've had about all the excitement you need for one evening, young man."

So William joined the fun at the good-bye party, still wearing his slightly damp tunic and telling everyone who asked, and almost believing it himself, that the only reason he'd been late was because he'd had a hard time getting his ears untangled.

So what happened then?" Jancy said. "Why didn't the sergeant arrest them and put them in jail?"

"I don't know if he could have caught up with them by the time he'd finished finding out if I was still alive," William answered. "I wasn't noticing much at the time, but afterward, Buddy told me that before Sergeant Blanding picked me up off the floor, he grabbed both of those Baggetts by the backs of their necks and threw them out the door, and they didn't even try to come back."

William and Jancy's conversation was taking place on the front steps of the cafeteria, while Aunt Fiona and Trixie were still at the table watching Buddy finish his big breakfast and talking to all the people who came over to say good-bye.

"By the time he made sure I was still alive," William went on, "those Baggetts were long gone. He told me he was going to go looking for them as soon as he got Buddy back to Aunt Fiona, but I told him not to bother."

"Why?" Jancy demanded, throwing up her hands in

exasperation. "Why on earth did you tell him that? He should have thrown them in jail. Both of them."

"Shh," William warned her as some people came out of the door. It turned out to be Tom and Virginia, and they stopped long enough to tell William good-bye again, and ask him to keep in touch. "I'll bet we'll be reading your name in neon before too long," Tom said. "I'm counting on it."

And William laughed and said, "Great. But don't hold your breath."

They both took the time to write down their addresses, and have William give them his Gold Beach one, while Jancy squirmed and poked William and whispered for him to hurry. But as soon as they left Jancy asked again, "Why on earth didn't you want the sergeant to arrest those thugs?"

William said he had to think about that for a minute, but down underneath he really knew why. If Sergeant Blanding had arrested the two Baggetts, there would have been a big fuss, and stuff in the papers and everything. And all the people he'd met at Mannsville would have had to know how he, William, was related to the two goons who had tried to rob him. And all sorts of other embarrassing Baggetty stuff would have had to come out.

But what William told Jancy was, "Well, what I said to Sergeant Blanding was that I didn't see the point, because they were probably halfway back to Crownfield by then. And since I'd be leaving Mannsville tomorrow, they wouldn't have any reason to come back. Not ever. That is . . ." He grinned at Jancy. "That is, unless seeing one performance of 𝕬 𝕸idsummer 𝕹ight's 𝕯ream turned them both into 𝕾hakespeare lovers."

She grinned back at him. "Not likely," she said.

"That's what I told the sergeant," William said. "When I said it wasn't likely they'd ever show up here again, he kind of agreed with me. So he said that as soon as he took Buddy back to Aunt Fiona, he'd make sure they weren't still around, and that would be the end of it. So I just went to the cast party, and after a little while Sergeant Blanding came back to get me and took me right to the door of the dormitory."

"But when he came to get you, didn't he tell the rest of the people at the party about the Baggetts and what they did to you?" Jancy asked.

"No, he surely didn't. I didn't tell him not to, but he seemed to know I didn't want him to. When he came back, he just told them he thought there'd been enough party time for someone my age. They kidded him about how he was acting like a daddy instead of a cop, but Miss Scott agreed with him. She said that either Mr. Turner had lightened the color of my greasepaint, or I was a little off-color. She said she thought it was because I needed a rest."

Jancy nodded. "That sounds like what Miss Scott would say. But it seems to me—"

William interrupted her. "But what I want to know is what Buddy told you and Aunt Fiona about what happened. It must have scared her half to death when he told her about the Baggetts showing up in my dressing room, and what they did to me."

Jancy's eyes widened. "You know what? He didn't say a word about it. He just said we took so long in the ladies' room he got tired of waiting, and there were so many people around he got himself lost. That's all he said. I wonder why."

William shook his head. "Gee, I don't know. Sergeant Blanding must have told him not to tell about the Baggetts because it would scare you and Aunt Fiona too much. But what I don't get is why Buddy did what he was told—for once in his life."

"I know." Jancy nodded. "It sure isn't like him. Except that . . ."

"Except what?"

"Well, I don't know exactly," Jancy said. "Except that Sergeant Blanding really made a big impression on him. All he talked about while we were putting him to bed last night was how big and strong the sergeant is. He kept saying the sergeant must be the goodest strong guy in the whole world. Not the strongest good guy. The goodest strong guy."

William laughed. "Maybe it just dawned on him that you can be a good guy even if you're strong as a horse."

Jancy sighed. "Well, it's about time he learned that."

They grinned at each other, but then she sighed again. "But what I'm still worrying about is, what will happen if the Baggetts decide to come after you again in Gold Beach? They might, you know. I guess they still think you're a millionaire." She scratched her head, making her hair into a curly halo. "Maybe we can have the Ogdens write them a letter explaining how come you're not rich and how they're going to get nothing but a whole lot of trouble if they show up in Gold Beach again."

William didn't think that was a great idea. "Look," he told Jancy. "Clarice has probably told her parents about whatever it was I did that made her so mad at me. So probably they're mad at me too."

"No, I don't think so," Jancy said. "After all, they're lawyers, and lawyers don't like it when people do unlawful stuff like Rudy and Gary were trying to do. So they'll probably want to help, even if Clarice doesn't." Jancy's eyes suddenly widened. Her voice got even lower. "Oh, I forgot to tell you. I talked to Clarice last night. In the ladies' room. And I think I know what you did that made her mad at you."

"You do? Well, I'd sure like to know. Tell me."

Jancy cocked her head. "Well, it wasn't so much what you did to *her*. She said you did something to someone else, though. Someone she liked a lot, I guess. His name is—"

A lightbulb went off in William's head. "Let me guess," he interrupted. "His name is Bernard?"

"Oh, you know? You already knew about him then? What did you do to him?"

William grinned. "Nothing, really. Except he wanted to be Puck and I got the part. But what I don't get is what changed. Before Clarice stopped speaking to me, she was saying that what we ought to do was tell on Bernard and get him in trouble because of what *he'd* done to *me*."

"To you? What did he do to you?"

"Oh, nothing much. Just tore up my promptbook and greased that vine I used to swing onstage, so I slid down and almost broke my ankle. And you know something else? The very last thing Clarice said, before she stopped talking to me, was that she'd told Bernard that we knew what he'd done. And right after that, she stopped speaking to me. What I can't figure out is what happened in between."

"Hmm," Jancy said. "Maybe I can. I'm going to work on it."

William laughed. "Swell. You do that. Because I'm not."

I t was right after breakfast, only a day or two after the Hardisons got back to Gold Beach, that William made his next journal entry.

> Well, here I am back in my room at 971
> Eleanor Street, and in just a few days I'll be
> starting my freshman year at Gold Beach High.
> I've been up to the school to register, and it
> doesn't look too bad. I mean, it has some pretty
> nice buildings. I got to meet Mr. Cutler, who's
> the principal, and a couple of other people. And
> Aunt Fiona says there are some really good
> teachers, for things like English and geometry.
> So it sounds kind of okay. No drama department,
> though, but you can't have everything. Right?
>     Anyway, in a year or two I might try to
> get a scholarship for a private boarding school
> that is especially for people who want to act.
> Miss Scott told me she'd be glad to write me a

*recommendation, and having been in a Mannsville production would help a lot.*

He stopped for a moment to think about that. And then he wrote: *Other news? Oh yes. The Clarice thing.*

He put down his pen. There had been a lot of recent twists and turns in what you might call the Clarice story. So many that writing it all down would be like a murder mystery story, where there were so many mixed-up clues that the author kept forgetting which one of the characters he was going to murder. And what made it even more confusing was that in this particular mystery, a lot of the recent clues were secondhand—by way of Jancy. Because ever since the Hardisons got back to Gold Beach, Jancy and Clarice had been writing to each other.

Jancy kept telling William she couldn't let him see her letters from Clarice because she'd promised Clarice she absolutely, positively wouldn't. So she didn't. But that didn't stop her from telling him what was in every one of them, down to the last word. For instance, how Clarice had written that as soon as she really got to know Bernard, she realized how unfair she and William had been to him.

"Gee!" William said when Jancy told him that. "She said I was unfair to Bernard?"

"Well," Jancy said, "what Clarice says is that Bernard only put the bacon grease on your entry rope so it wouldn't be so scratchy on your hands, and he didn't know it would make you fall. And he also told her he wasn't the one who tore up your little notebook. He said somebody did it who was mad at you for being an upstager. And the only reason those scraps were lying there under his jacket was because he had been collecting them to take home and see if he could paste them all back together."

When Jancy told him that, William slapped his forehead in amazement. "*Sure* he did," he said. "Jancy. You're telling me that Clarice fell for a bunch of lies like that?"

"I know. It doesn't seem possible," Jancy said. "But she said she really did believe him. Well, what she actually wrote was that she really did believe him for a while, but maybe not anymore. Not lately."

"The thing is," Jancy went on, "in her last letter she said that she guessed that what made her believe Bernard's story in the first place was . . ." Jancy rolled her eyes, grinned, and clasped her hands over her heart. "It was because she was in *love*."

At first William didn't get it at all. If Clarice was in love with him, like Jancy was always telling him, why would that make her believe Bernard's lies? But all of a sudden he began to get it. "So," he said, "you mean Clarice is in love with Bernard now?"

Jancy began to nod, then stopped nodding and shook her head. "Not exactly. Not anymore, anyway. What she said in this last letter was that she *was* in love with Bernard for a while. But she's not anymore."

William slapped his forehead even harder. "Wow!" he said. And then, grinning, he added, "So who's she in love with now?" He thought he was making a joke, but Jancy's answer was absolutely serious. "Well, his name is Alfred. His family just moved to Gardenia Street, and he has big muscles and curly hair."

William thought about that for a minute or two before he got up to go. "Oh. Well, okay. I guess I get it, at least sort of," he said. But Jancy grabbed his arm and stopped him.

She had a worried look on her face as she asked, "Are you sorry that Clarice doesn't love you anymore?"

William's answer was, "No. Of course not. I never believed it anyway." That's what he told Jancy, but after he gave it some more thought, he decided that what he'd said wasn't entirely true. Thinking a girl was in love with you was kind of interesting, but if it ever happened again, he hoped the person who loved him didn't change her mind quite as often.

So that was about where the Clarice story stood at present, and thinking it over, William decided not to even try to put the whole thing—or even any part of it— down in pen and ink. Learning to understand females, he decided, was another project, along with keeping Buddy from turning into a real Baggett, that he was going to have to work on right away. Like before school started, when he would probably be too busy.

Putting his journal away, he went downstairs to see if he could find something less complicated than the female thing to begin with—like, for instance, finding Buddy and making sure he wasn't picking the neighbors' flowers, or beating up on their kids.

Yes, he told himself, he really needed to think about Buddy. The thing was, after having a tendency to not take the Buddy problem too seriously when Jancy was writing to him about it, something had happened on the long drive home from Mannsville that made him reconsider. But of course he couldn't discuss it with Jancy at the time. Not with all five Hardisons and a lot of luggage crammed into Aunt Fiona's Dodge.

Up until then he'd been shrugging it off by telling himself that Jancy was just a natural-born worrier, but that afternoon in the car, he happened to be thinking about the problem when he noticed Buddy drawing an imaginary line with his finger between his part of the backseat and Trixie's. He had a Baggetty expression on his face as he drew the line and then, still scowling, he leaned over and said something in Trixie's ear.

When William asked Buddy what he'd just said to Trixie, he clamped his mouth shut and shook his head. But then Trixie said, "Ask me. Ask me, William." And when he did, she said, "He said that if I put one single finger on his side of that line, he'd bite it off and throw it out the window. Didn't you, Buddy? Didn't you say that?" Buddy's frown got even fiercer, but he didn't deny it.

That was what made William start to wonder if Jancy had been right all along. He decided right then he was going to have a serious discussion on the subject with Jancy, and maybe later with Aunt Fiona, too, as soon as possible.

However, when they finally reached Gold Beach, there was so much to do, settling into his room again and getting unpacked, and getting used to being a part of the Hardison family of Gold Beach again, instead of the bigshot actor of the Mannsville Shakespeare Festival, that it was a few days before he remembered the talk he'd meant to have with Jancy about the Buddy problem.

He wasn't looking forward to it, but that particular afternoon Aunt Fiona had gone to the grocery store and had taken Buddy and Trixie with her, so it seemed like a good time.

He went looking for Jancy and found her in the backyard, sitting under the oak tree, reading a book. When she looked up, he asked her what she was reading, and she said it was *Huckleberry Finn*.

"Well," he said, "I'd hate to interrupt Mark Twain, and I'm not in that big of a hurry to discuss it, but I guess we'd better talk about Buddy the Baggett. You know, like you kept writing about, when I was in Mannsville?"

Jancy put her finger in her book to save her place and looked up at him. "Well, okay," she said, nodding thoughtfully. "But you know what? I haven't been worrying about that as much. Not lately. Not since we got home from Mannsville, anyway."

William was kind of surprised. Actually, it didn't seem to him that Buddy had improved all that much. He still wasn't eating his vegetables, and yesterday he'd punched out two different neighbor kids, one right after the other. So William reminded Jancy about the punched noses, not to mention how, just last night, he'd sassed Aunt Fiona when she told him to eat his peas.

"Yes, I know," Jancy said. "He's still pretty awful. But something that happened in Mannsville made me realize that, bad as he is, we won't ever need to worry about Buddy growing up to be an honest-to-goodness Baggett."

"Really." William was once again thinking how hard it was to understand women, when he suddenly began to guess what had changed Jancy's mind. "Oh, you mean because of how he saved my neck when Rudy and Gary were giving me a bad time?"

"Yes, that's part of it. That was a good thing. But I'm not just talking about being good. The important thing was *how* he did it."

"How he did it?" William asked. "What do you mean? All he did was go out and get Sergeant Blanding."

"Exactly," Jancy said.

Yes." Jancy was grinning. "That's the important part. How Buddy did it! What did he do when Rudy and Gary showed up? Instead of just trying to fight them, which would have been good of him all right—but pretty dumb—he ran right out and got a *policeman*. Just think about that for a minute, William," she went on. "Would any honest-to-goodness Baggett ever go *looking for the police*?"

After he'd thought about it, William wasn't too sure that solved the Buddy problem, but he was glad Jancy thought so.

So he grinned at her and said, "Okay. You might be right."

A little later William went back to his room, thinking that his life had suddenly calmed down quite a bit. For one thing, Clarice didn't seem to be *his* problem anymore, and for another, Jancy had stopped trying to get him all worked up about Buddy. Two big problems more or less solved, at least for the present. *And* there were still a few more days before school began. So right at the moment, he wasn't as busy as usual, and there wasn't even that much to worry about. Which meant, it suddenly occurred to him, that it just might be a good time for William **S.** Hardison, experienced **Shakespearean** actor, to start deciding what new role he might start rehearsing.

But then came dinner, so it wasn't until quite a bit later that he found time to go through his **Doubleday's Complete Works** looking for a future role. It was a hot night, and he opened the window and stripped down to his undershorts before he began his search. Sitting cross-legged on his bed, with the big volume on a pillow on his lap, he started by checking out **Twelfth Night.**

A lot of time had passed, and a lot had happened since he started reading about the Duke and Viola and Sir Toby Belch, but he remembered liking what he'd read. But when he went over the list of characters, or the Dramatis Personae, as **Doubleday** called it, he couldn't find any character that a smallish—okay, slightly scrawny—not-quite-fourteen-year-old would be good typecasting for.

After some thought he got off the bed and went to the mirror. Leaning close, he checked out his "gorgeous eyes," "great cheekbones," and "electric smile." Of course, it had only been Clarice who'd said that about his eyes, right before she stopped talking to him and fell in love with Bernard. But that stuff about his cheekbones and smile had come from Mr. Turner, his dresser and makeup artist, who didn't seem to be the type to say things and then change his mind.

So far so good. But when he went on to raise his fists and flex his muscles in an Atlas pose, what he saw wasn't as promising. After a minute he grinned ruefully and told himself that was another problem he'd have to work on.

Back on the bed he began to check out a few of the other plays that were on Miss Scott's reading list. He read through several Dramatis Personae, but he couldn't find any other sprites or hobgoblins or even a half-grown gentleman.

There was a clown in As You Like It. A clown could be made up and padded so you couldn't tell much about what shape the person under the costume was in. So that was a possibility, but not a very good one, since gorgeous eyes and great cheekbones wouldn't count for much. He went on flipping pages.

It was on page 313 that he came across Romeo and Juliet. That stopped him for a while. He'd read parts of it before, and Miss Scott had discussed it in class. She'd said it was one of her favorites, and of course it was probably Shakespeare's most famous play. Not that your less-than-average-size almost-fourteen-year-old would be good typecasting for a handsome, sword-fighting ladies' man, but someday, who knows?

William skimmed several acts, pausing now and then to try out a few of Romeo's lines and consider how he might say them.

It wasn't all that easy. Romeo, William decided, tended to beat around the bush an awful lot. It wasn't until near the end of the play that he came to the place where Romeo drinks the poison. That seemed to offer more possibilities.

Imagining an ancient, dust-encrusted bottle, William pretended to uncork it. Sniffing its contents, he recoiled in disgust. Steeling himself, clenching his teeth, squinting his eyes, and jutting his chin, he brought the bottle to his lips once more—closed his eyes, slowly forced his lips to open—and drank.

Shuddering and clutching his throat, William S. Hardison, experienced actor, gurgled, "'O true apothecary! / Thy drugs are quick. Thus with a kiss I die.'"

After that line, the stage direction said only Dies, but William padded his part, like Mr. Andre had done so often in A Midsummer Night's Dream. Staggering around the room clutching his throat, he returned to embrace and passionately kiss a vividly evoked Juliet more than once, before he keeled over, convulsed dramatically, did it again, and finally went limp.

He was getting to his feet when he suddenly remembered something else he'd meant to do that evening. He looked at his watch, wondering if it was too late to phone

Charlie and ask him if he'd like to practice backflips and handstands tomorrow in his dad's barn.

Eight o'clock. No, that wasn't too late. Putting **Doubleday's Complete Works** on the shelf—for the time being—he headed for the phone.

Start at the beginning of the adventure
with *William S. and the Great Escape.*

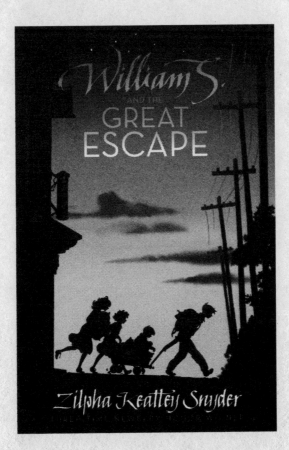

**H**is birth certificate, if he even had one, probably just said Willy Baggett, but for most of the seventh grade he'd been signing his school papers William S. Baggett.

## William 𝒮. Baggett

But that, too, would change as soon as he made his move. No more Baggett then—and good riddance.

Actually, he'd started thinking about running away almost seven years ago. That was when he'd started going to school and began to learn, among other things, that not everybody behaved like Baggetts. And not very long after that he began putting every penny he could get his hands on into what he thought of as his Getaway Fund. Well, not quite every penny. He did spend a dime, now and then, on a Saturday matinee at the Roxie Theater. Watching how your favorite movie actors could make you believe they were all those different people was one thing he'd never been able to do without.

In spite of an occasional movie, his secret stash had grown pretty fast while the Baggetts still lived in the city, where there were lots of lawns to mow and flower gardens to water and weed. And even after they had to get out of town, he'd managed to add a few coins now and then by doing odd jobs at school—carrying stuff for teachers, and mopping up on rainy days for Mr. Jenkins, the janitor.

He'd made other plans and preparations too. Besides saving his earnings, he began to keep a long, narrow knapsack beside his bed, and all his most important belongings right there within arm's reach, ready to push into it. And then, someday, he would take his Getaway Fund out of its supersecret, hard-to-reach hiding place, sling his knapsack over his shoulder, and simply walk away. And that would be that.

But what then? Where would he run to? Over the years he'd changed his mind a lot, but just recently he'd come up with some interesting possibilities. Like, how about Hollywood? Or Broadway in New York City? Or even better, Stratford-upon-Avon. Okay, not likely. But, "We are such stuff as dreams are made on." Right?

He never told anyone, of course. Not even Jancy, at least not until after she'd pretty much guessed. But the little bit Jancy knew didn't worry him that much.

His sister would never do anything to ruin his future career. He was sure of that. Well, he *had* been sure anyway, until the day her guinea pig got flushed down the toilet, which not only messed up the plumbing, but apparently changed everything.

Sweetie Pie had been Jancy's pet ever since her fourth-grade teacher got tired of a health class experiment that involved feeding some guinea pigs fruits and vegetables, and some others nothing but candy and cookies. Sweetie Pie had been one of the stunted sweet-stuff pigs, and she never quite made it to normal guinea pig size. Not even after Jancy went to the trouble to clear off a stretch of cluttered, weed-grown land to plant a vegetable garden. She did manage to grow a little bit of healthy stuff for Sweetie Pie, and she would have grown a lot more if Gary and the twins hadn't decided to use her garden plot as one end of their football field.

Even though Sweetie Pie never got much bigger, she was, according to Jancy, the smartest, cutest guinea pig that ever lived. But then came the first of August, 1938, and Sweetie Pie's story came to a sad end.

William found out about it soon after it happened, when he overheard the twins snickering outside the bathroom door. What he heard them saying was how they'd managed to "get rid of that stinkin' rat, and let Buddy take the rap."

William wanted to pound on the door and yell at

them—not that that would have accomplished anything, except getting himself beaten to a pulp. Besides being extra big for fourteen-year-olds, Al and Andy were extra vicious. So William bit his lip and went looking for Jancy.

For a while he couldn't find her anywhere. Not in the room she shared with Trixie and Buddy, and not anywhere else in the big old wreck of a house. Not hiding behind any of the junkyard furniture in what might once have been a pretty nice living room, or out on the halfway collapsed veranda, either. But then, as he was checking the back hall, there she was, walking toward her room with her mop of hair hiding her face as usual. But when she saw him, she put her finger in her ear—their secret signal that asked for a talk in their private hideout.

Okay, fine. No amount of talk was going to do poor Sweetie Pie any good at that point, but William knew how Jancy must be feeling, and if talking would help, he was ready to listen. Ready and willing, even though it meant making a feverish (hay feverish, that is) trip to the barn—the huge, saggy-roofed building that sat about fifty yards from the condemned farmhouse where the Baggetts had been hanging out ever since they got more or less kicked out of downtown Crownfield.

Nowadays the barn was a kind of junkyard where all the Baggetts who were old enough to drive—not to mention the ones who drove even though they weren't old enough—had stashed the body parts of a whole lot of dead hot rods, pickup trucks, and motorcycles. Down there on the ground floor the scene was nothing but rusty carcasses, but up above the car cemetery there was a secret place that nobody seemed to know about except William and Jancy. A deserted area that must have been a hayloft back in the days when the huge old building had been a cow barn instead of a car dump.

So a moldy hayloft had become their favorite place to have a really private conversation, in spite of what it always did to William's hay fever. He didn't mind that much about the hay fever thing. Being forced to choose between being teased and tormented or having hay fever wasn't nearly the worst thing about being at the bottom of the Baggett pecking order.

On the plus side, the loft was fairly handy. All it took was a well-timed scamper across the cluttered yard to the barn door. And then a careful zigzag around and over fractured fenders and rusty radiators until you got to a narrow ladder that led up to a place where you could scrunch down behind a big pile of moldy hay and be fairly sure none of the bigger Baggetts would show up.

Up behind the haystack, in between William's sneezing and sniffing fits, he and Jancy had now and then managed to come up with the kind of plans that were necessary in order to survive as comparatively small and defenseless Baggetts. Plans like how to discourage Gary from throwing your books off the bus on the way to school, or where to hide your most precious possessions where Al and Andy couldn't get at them. So it was up there in the hayloft that William was waiting when Jancy's curly head and red, weepy eyes appeared over the edge of the loft floor.

The weepy eyes were no surprise. But what he certainly hadn't foreseen was how the conversation began. The very first words out of Jancy's mouth were, "Look here, William, I know you're getting ready to run away. You are, aren't you?"

Puzzled, William shrugged. "Well, yeah, I guess so. Sooner or later. Why?"

He was still wondering what his plans for the future had to do with the sad fate of Sweetie Pie, when Jancy cleared that up by explaining that she had decided that what happened to Sweetie Pie was the last straw.

"I'm just plain finished with being a Baggett," she told William fiercely. "So I'm going to run away too, as soon as ever I can."

William was shocked. "What are you talking about?" he said. "You're only eleven years old. A little kid like you can't just take off all by yourself."

Jancy threw up her hands. "Listen to me, William," she said. "I didn't mean all by myself. I said *too*. Like, with you. And it has to be real soon. Like maybe tomorrow. Don't you get it?"

William got it, but he didn't like it. However, he knew from experience that when Jancy really made her mind up about certain kinds of things that was pretty much it—not much use to argue. But he kept trying.

"But the problem is," he insisted, "I'm not ready yet. Look at me, Jancy. I'm just a kid." He shrugged and screwed up his face in the kind of lopsided smile that an actor uses to show he's joking—mostly joking, anyway. "Well okay, a supersmart and talented person, maybe, but still just a twelve-year-old kid." He was kidding, but not entirely. He was pretty smart, all right. No Baggett, not even the ones who put him down as a smart aleck and teacher's pet, could deny that.

And as for talented? Well, according to Miss Scott . . . But that was another story. The only story he had to come up with right now was one that would keep Jancy from running away. At least for a few more years.

"The kind of help you'd need for a successful getaway," he told her, "is somebody with a lot more than just smarts. Like, what you're going to need is some big, musclebound type guy."

Trying for a laugh—Jancy usually liked comedy—he stuck out his skinny chest and flexed invisible muscles.

No laugh. Jancy listened, squinty eyed and silent. He sighed. Even though she'd known about his running-away plan for a long time, she also knew, or should have, that he'd always seen it as something that was going to happen in the fairly distant future. And now, suddenly, it was like *right this minute?*

Things were moving way too fast. It wasn't more than an hour since the Sweetie Pie tragedy, and now Jancy was jumping the gun by announcing that she'd never been cut out to be a Baggett, and she was going to prove it by running away.

"Okay. Running away to where?" William asked. "Where you planning to go?"

Jancy raised her head and jutted her small pointed chin. "To Gold Beach," she said firmly. "I'm going to go to Gold Beach to live with our aunt Fiona."

William shook his head doubtfully. "I wouldn't count on it," he said. Fiona Hardison, their mother's sister, was a schoolteacher who lived in a little town on the northern California coast. A woman whom William and Jancy had met only once, right after their mother died, and that was four long years ago. "What makes you think Aunt Fiona would let you live with her?" William asked.

"Oh, she will," Jancy said. "She'll be so happy to get Trixie and Buddy back, she'll be glad to have you and me, too."

And that was how Jancy finally got around to mentioning an important minor detail. Not only would William and Jancy be running away together—they were going to be taking Trixie and Buddy with them.

Under the circumstances, Jancy's decision to give up on being a Baggett wasn't all that surprising. After all, she'd probably loved poor old Sweetie Pie more than any Baggett, except possibly William himself—and the two little kids, of course.

That was another thing about Jancy. She'd liked little things, the littler the better. Not that William, who was actually a year and a half older and a couple of inches taller than she was, could play that role very well. He wasn't really little, but according to popular opinion (Baggett opinion anyway), pretty much of a wimp. So maybe that's what made the difference with Jancy. William was aware that little and cute was way out ahead where Jancy was concerned, but skinny and wimpy might come in a close second.

That day in the hayloft, William's arguments got even more frantic after Jancy mentioned that her escape plan included Trixie and Buddy. "Holy Toledo, Jancy," he said, when she let that minor detail slip out. "You can't be serious. And I'll tell you right now that I am *very* serious about not helping commit a double kidnapping. You know what they do to kidnappers when they catch them. Like that guy who stole the Lindbergh baby. Zap!" He did an exaggerated quivering, stiff-limbed impression of an electric chair victim. Still no smile. He shrugged. "Anyway, I mean it. Count me out."

"But you told me——," Jancy was beginning when he interrupted.

"Okay, so I did say I was going to clear out, and I meant it. But I meant later. Like when I'm practically an adult. Like fourteen or fifteen. Not now, when I won't even be thirteen till next month. And as for you getting those two little kids all the way to Gold Beach? No way. Doing it all by yourself? I mean, look at you."

She did, and William did too. There she was, barely eleven years old, and small for her age. And at the moment—it was a blazing hot day—wearing one of Babe's outgrown sundresses. On Babe, who was fifteen, the dress had looked—well, kind of sexy, in a not very classy way. But on Jancy's skinny little stick of a body, it only made her look like the wrong end of a hard winter.

With the hay fever kicking in pretty badly, William had to stop to sneeze several times before he went on. "So I'm supposed to believe that what I'm looking at right this minute is a dangerous kidnapper who's going to nab two little kids and get them all the way to Gold Beach without getting caught? More than a hundred miles from here? And even if you managed to get that far before the police caught up with you, what makes you think Aunt Fiona would let you stay? She didn't even answer the last time you wrote to her."

"I know," Jancy said. "But she did write me two letters that were all about how awful bad she felt when Big Ed took Buddy and Trixie away. Like how she'd had them and loved them for two years and would have kept them forever if Big Ed hadn't showed up all of a sudden to take them back."

"Yeah, I *know*," William said. "I remember." What he knew, and would never forget, was that right after Buddy was born, their mother, Laura Hardison Baggett, died. Died very suddenly, leaving behind newborn Buddy and two-year-old Trixie to be taken care of by Big Ed and a bunch of Baggett teenagers. William had been eight years old at the time, and he remembered that final scene all too well. Especially when he was trying not to.

Back then Big Ed had been glad to let Aunt Fiona take Buddy and Trixie away to live with her. Let them go probably because there was no longer any Baggett left alive who was willing and able to change diapers. William had been willing to try, and he'd said so, but nobody would listen to him. So the two youngest Baggetts went to live with their mother's sister, who kept them for two years before Big Ed decided to take them back.

That happened right after he'd married Gertie, his third wife. What Big Ed told the welfare people was that he took the two little kids back because Gertie wanted to be a mother to them. As far as William could see, Gertie wasn't, and never had been, the least bit interested in being a mother to anyone. The way William figured, it was a lot more likely that President Roosevelt's new welfare plan had something to do with Big Ed's decision to have all his kids under the same roof. The New Deal plan that gave really poor families a certain amount of money for each of their children.

"Aunt Fiona probably didn't answer your letter," William told Jancy, "because she was sure that if she got them back, Big Ed would just show up and grab them away again."

"I know." Jancy hung her head so that a bunch of her thick, streaky-blond hair swung down, hiding her small face. Jancy got teased about her hair—got called Mop Head and Rabbit Tail and even worse names. Actually, William thought her curly hair was her best feature, at least when it was clean and combed, which wasn't all that often. He'd told her so before, but now he said nothing at all, and after a while she said, "I know" again, in a faint weepy voice. "But I am leaving, for absolute sure and certain, and I just can't leave the poor little things here all alone."

"Humph!" William snorted. "All alone? Not hardly.

Even with you gone, and maybe me too, that still leaves—let's see." He pretended to count on his fingers. "Seven"—he stopped to sneeze—"that leaves eight big Baggetts, if you count Gertie."

"Yeah, exactly," Jancy said. "That's exactly why I can't leave Trixie and Buddy here."

William got her point, and he couldn't help but agree, but just then another thought hit him. "I don't get it. What I don't get is why you'd *want* to bother with them. Well, Trixie maybe." He could sort of understand that. Trixie was kind of hard to resist. "But Buddy? I mean, wasn't he the one who flushed the toilet?"

Her face still hidden by her hair, Jancy nodded. "I know," she kind of gasped. And when she went on, her voice sounded wobbly. "But it wasn't his fault. Not really. Al, or else it was Andy—Buddy never can tell them apart—told him that a toilet is just the right size for a guinea pig bathtub, and when you flush, it's just like a guinea pig washing machine. It was that crummy twin's fault. I know it was awful dumb of Buddy to believe him, but he's only four years old. And who's going to tell him what else to not believe after both of us leave?"

William could tell she was crying by the sound of her voice, even though a heavy hunk of hair was hiding her face. "Crying won't do any good," he said.

But of course it did. After a few minutes of listening to her sobs and watching her skinny little shoulders shaking and quivering, he sighed and said, "Okay, okay. I'll think about it." And he meant it, even though it didn't take much thought to figure out that one reason, even the main reason, that Jancy wanted him to run away too was because she knew about—

"Oh thank you, thank you, William." Jancy interrupted his suspicious musings. And then her special talent for mind reading—at least where William was concerned— kicked in. "And it's not either because of your money," she said. "All that money in your running-away piggy bank."

William's snort was even louder. "My Getaway Fund is *not* in a piggy bank," he said.

"Well, whatever you keep it in," Jancy said quickly. "It's not because of your money. It's because you don't belong here either. You're not like the rest of them. You're not nearly as mean, and ever so much smarter and . . ."

William didn't have to listen to know the rest of what Jancy had to say. He'd heard her say it before when she wanted to get something out of him. But he also felt pretty sure that she said it because she knew it was true—at least the part about being smarter. But he still had a strong suspicion that his running-away money had a lot to do with it.

He shrugged. "Well, okay then, maybe I'm in. So what are your plans? I mean like *when*—and *how?*"

"When?" Jancy's smile, still tear wet, was wide and

beaming. "Well, as soon as ever I can. Tomorrow or else the next day, for sure." She nodded again, so hard her curly mop bounced up and down. "Not a minute later."

"Ookaaay," William drawled the word out slowly. "But then comes *how*. How are you going to do it?"

"Well," Jancy's big eyes rolled thoughtfully. "I guess I'll just . . ." Her voice trailed off to a whisper and then came slowly back. "Well, I'll just pack up all their clothes"—long pause—"and something to eat on the way, and then . . ."

"Yeah," William prompted. "And then?"

Jancy's bony little face widened into a wobbly smile. "And then you'll decide what to do. You will, won't you, William?"

William shoved to the back of his mind a lot of troublesome unanswered questions concerning such things as *how* and *when*, and the even more serious one about what Aunt Fiona's reaction might be to their unannounced arrival. He sneezed again, wiped his nose on his sleeve, sighed, and said, "Yeah. Well, sort of looks like I'll have to."